CHAPTER 21

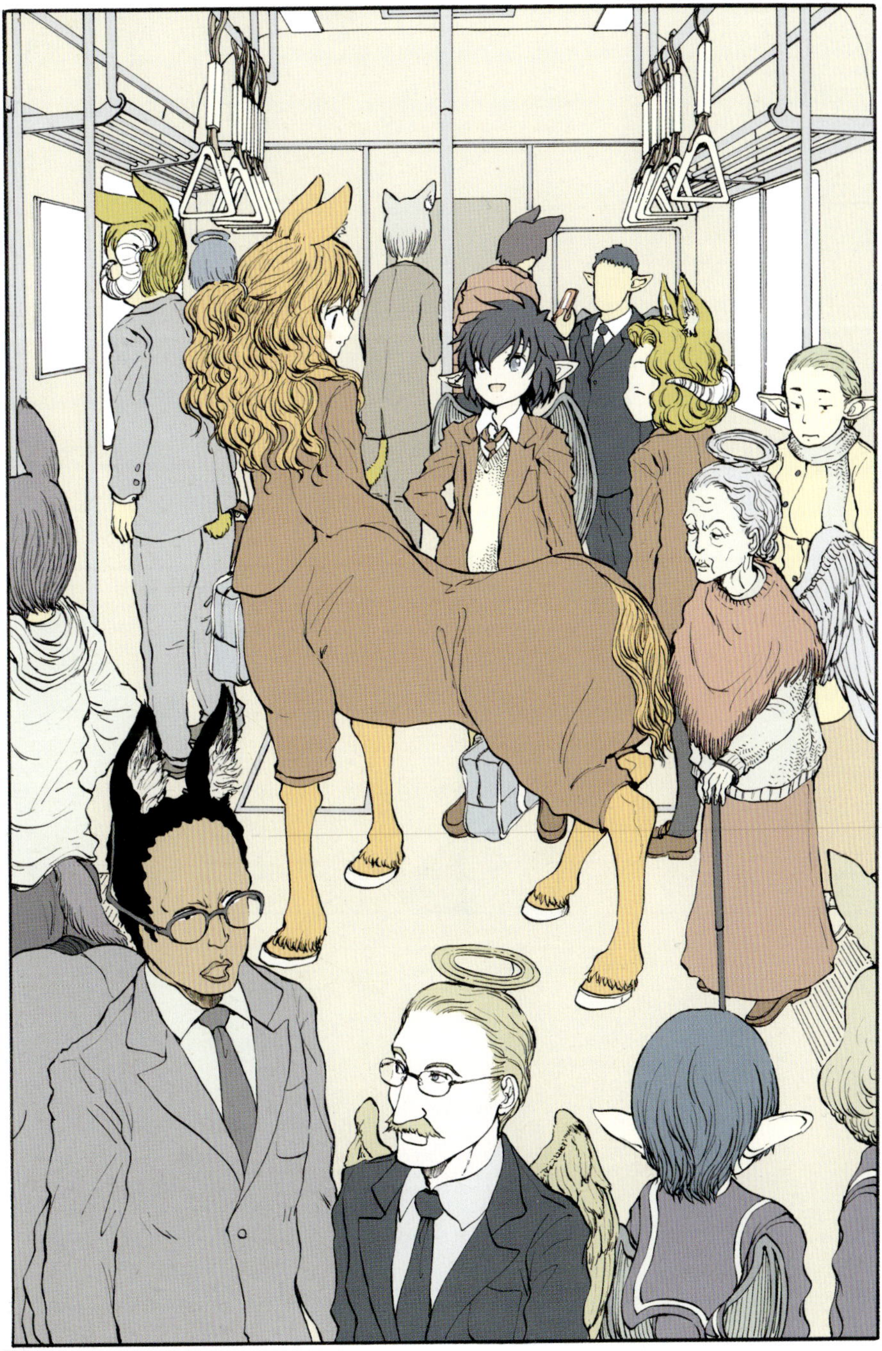

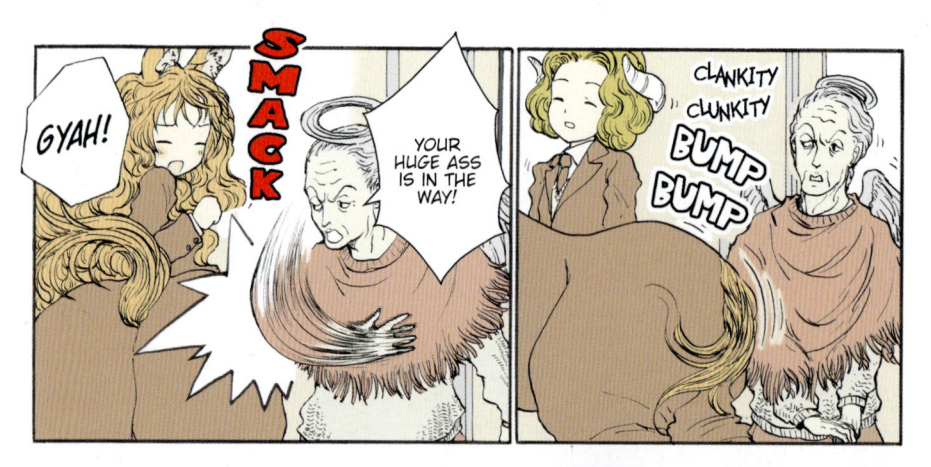

GYAH! **SMACK**	CLANKITY CLUNKITY **BUMP BUMP**
YOUR HUGE ASS IS IN THE WAY!	

Animals?!

MOTHER-IN-LAW!

SEATS GET BLOCKED AND THE ELDERLY HAVE IT SO **ROUGH**.

ANIMALS LIKE THIS RIDING THE TRAIN ARE THE REASON...

JAPAN IS SUCH A BACKWATER COUNTRY.

ALL HUMANS ARE ANIMALS TOO, SO SHE MEANT--!

Mmmrgh!

UM, SHE DIDN'T MEAN IT LIKE THAT...!

Imakanata! Imakanata!

DRAG DRAG

I'm **done** protecting your mother from her own racist comments!

You'd just abandon her?!

We have a **child** to think about!

What do you think you're doing?! You're just the daughter-in-law!

CARELESSLY SOWING SO MANY SEEDS FOR CONFLICT. THERE REALLY **IS** SOMETHING WRONG WITH HOW THAT GENERATION SEES THINGS.

THAT'S ILLEGAL, THOUGH.

OLD GEEZERS AND HAGS ARE LIKE THAT SOMETIMES.

It's racial discrimination.

HEY, DID YOU KNOW THERE'S EVIDENCE THAT ANCIENT SUMERIANS COMPLAINED ABOUT YOUNG PEOPLE FIVE THOUSAND YEARS AGO?

Always lecturing.

PEOPLE LIKE THAT ALWAYS COMPLAIN ABOUT "KIDS THESE DAYS."

EVEN THE STUFF THEY SAY HASN'T CHANGED AT ALL.

THEY SAID THE YOUTH DIDN'T KNOW ANYTHING AND DID NOTHING BUT LOITER IN TOWN.

CHATTER CHATTER

WELL, THINGS **ARE** GETTING BETTER... SLOWLY, BUT SURELY.

I THINK IT'S HARD FOR PEOPLE TO CHANGE.

A Centaur's Life
Vol. 5

story & art
KEI MURAYAMA

SEVEN SEAS ENTERTAINMENT PRESENTS

A Centaur's Life
story and art by KEI MURAYAMA
VOLUME 5

TRANSLATION
Angela Liu
Greg Moore

ADAPTATION
Holly Kolodziejczak

LETTERING AND LAYOUT
Jennifer Skarupa

LOGO DESIGN
Courtney Williams

COVER DESIGN
Nicky Lim

PROOFREADER
Patrick King

MANAGING EDITOR
Adam Arnold

PUBLISHER
Jason DeAngelis

CENTAUR NO NAYAMI VOLUME 5
© KEI MURAYAMA 2013
Originally published in Japan in 2013 by TOKUMA SHOTEN PUBLISHING CO., LTD., Tokyo. English translation rights arranged with TOKUMA SHOTEN PUBLISHING CO., LTD., Tokyo, through TOHAN CORPORATION, Tokyo.

No portion of this book may be reproduced or transmitted in any form without written permission from the copyright holders. This is a work of fiction. Names, characters, places, and incidents are the products of the author's imagination or are used fictitiously. Any resemblance to actual events, locals, or persons, living or dead, is entirely coincidental.

Seven Seas books may be purchased in bulk for educational, business, or promotional use. For information on bulk purchases, please contact Macmillan Corporate & Premium Sales Department at 1-800-221-7945 (ext 5442) or write specialmarkets@macmillan.com.

Seven Seas and the Seven Seas logo are trademarks of Seven Seas Entertainment, LLC. All rights reserved.

ISBN: 978-1-626921-11-5

Printed in Canada

First Printing: February 2015

10 9 8 7 6 5 4 3 2 1

FOLLOW US ONLINE: www.gomanga.com

READING DIRECTIONS

This book reads from *right to left*, Japanese style. If this is your first time reading manga, you start reading from the top right panel on each page and take it from there. If you get lost, just follow the numbered diagram here. It may seem backwards at first, but you'll get the hang of it! Have fun!!

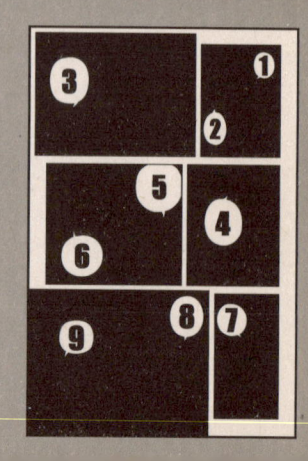

CHAPTER 22

YAY! A WALK! A WALK~!

WE WILL!

BE HOME BEFORE DARK!

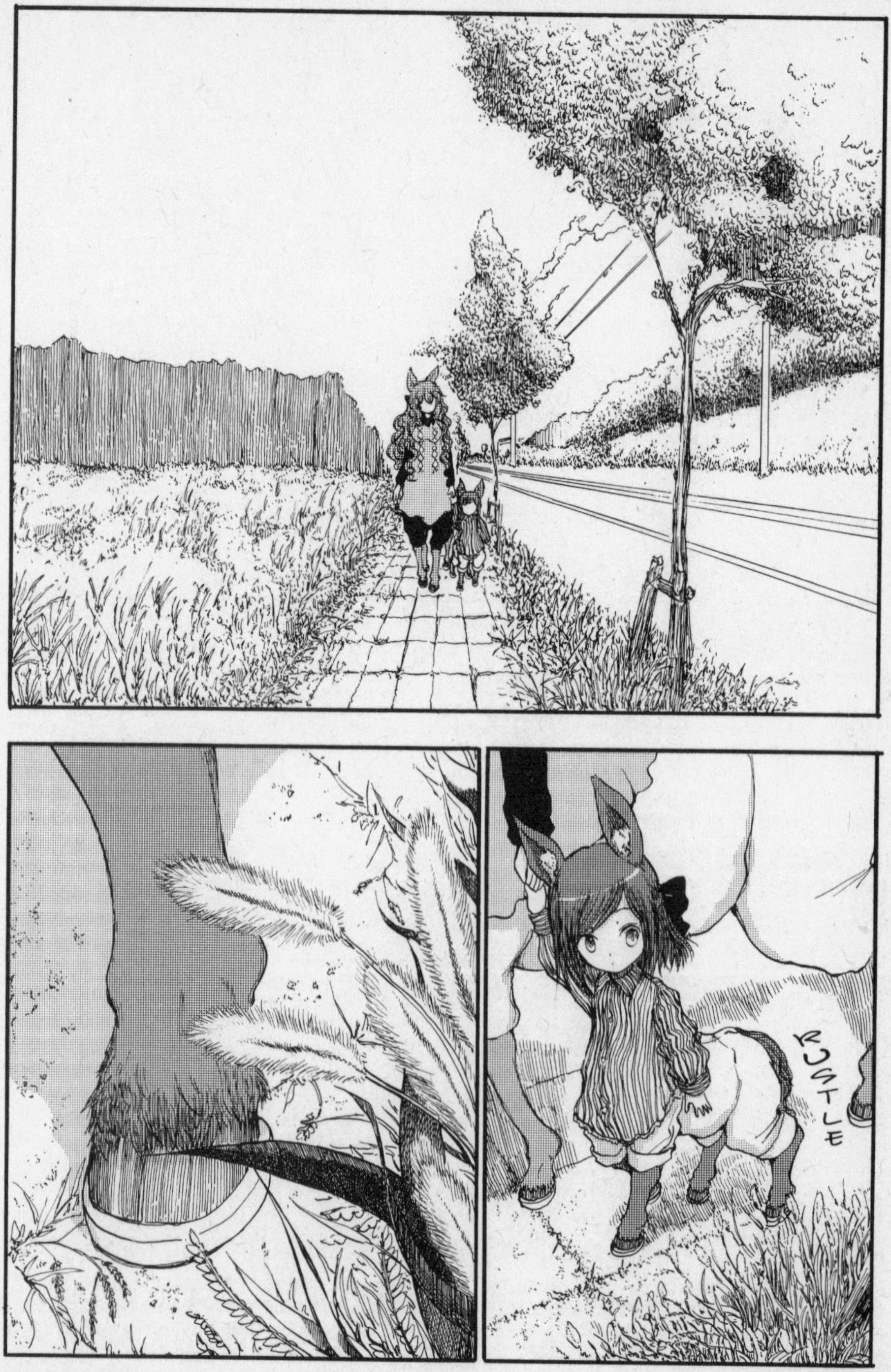
RUSTLE

BIG SIS! BIG SIS!
THERE'S A LOT OF GRASS!
YES, THERE IS.
IS ALL GRASS THE SAME?
NO, IT'S NOT.
WILD GRASSES HAVE THEIR OWN PROPER NAMES.

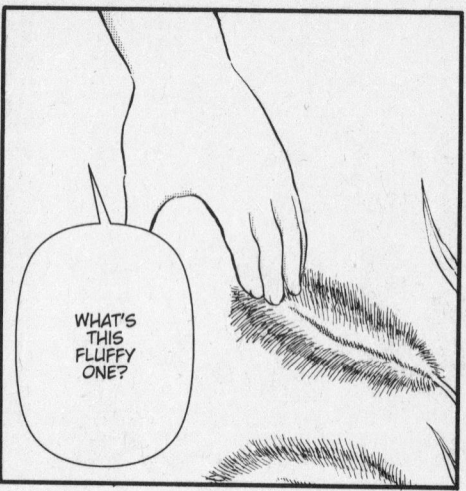

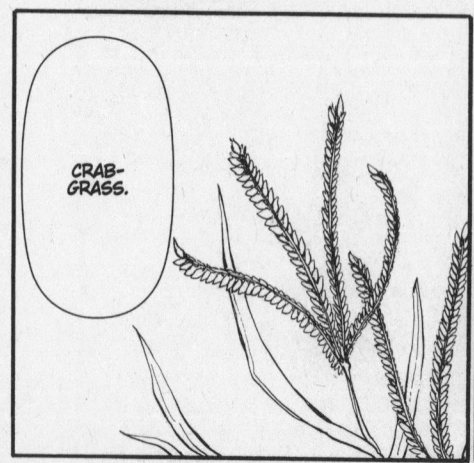

WHAT'S THIS FLUFFY ONE?

OH, THAT'S BRISTLEGRASS.

Bristlegrass...

AND THAT CHANGED TO BRISTLEGRASS.

IT KIND OF LOOKS LIKE A PUPPY'S TAIL, SO IT WAS ORIGINALLY CALLED DOGTAIL.

CRABGRASS.

WHAT ABOUT THIS ONE?

EARLIER IN THE SEASON, IT BLOOMS WITH YELLOW FLOWERS IN THE MORNING.

AND THIS ONE?

EVENING PRIMROSE.

RED CLOVER.

RED FLOWERS, THAT'S A...

DAISIES.

SMALL WITH WHITE FLOWERS...

CREEPING WOODSORREL.

SOW THISTLE.

HEY! BOYS USE THIS TO SWORDFIGHT EACH OTHER!

YEP, CANADA GOLDENROD.

DOES EVERYTHING HERE HAVE A NAME?

YES. EVEN THE SMALLEST GRASS AND FLOWER HAS A NAME.

DO THEY REALLY ALL HAVE NAMES?
WELL, THERE MIGHT BE A FEW THAT STILL DON'T.
IF YOU FIND ONE THAT DOESN'T HAVE A NAME, YOU GET TO NAME IT, SHINO.
REALLY?!
THEN, THEN, I'LL NAME IT AFTER BIG SISTER, MOMMY, AND DADDY!
THEN, AUNTIE, UNCLE, GRANDPA, GRANDMA, AND MAKI-CHAN!
WE'RE HOME~!
HERE YOU GO. THIS IS THE BOOK WITH NAMES OF GRASS.
LUG
Nngh!
Ummph!
THERE SURE ARE A LOT OF NAMES AND A LOT OF KANJI!
YUP... THAT THERE ARE.

A Centaur's Life

MESOZOIC CREATURES

DINOSAURS & THEIR CLOSE RELATIVES: THE DAWN OF THE AGE OF DINOSAURS

WHEN IT COMES TO MUSEUM EXHIBITS, DINOSAURS ARE ALWAYS INCREDIBLY POPULAR. THOSE MONSTROUS MONOLITHS OF RESTORED BONE HAVE ALWAYS GENERATED TREMENDOUS INTEREST. BUT JUST WHAT KINDS OF CREATURES WERE THESE DINOSAURS, ANYWAY? AND HOW DID THEY DIFFER FROM THE REPTILES WE SEE TODAY?

DINOSAURS WERE CREATURES THAT LIVED DURING THE MESOZOIC ERA (APPROXIMATELY 252 MILLION TO 66 MILLION YEARS AGO) AND WERE MEMBERS OF THE SAME GROUP OF ANIMALS AS LIZARDS, CROCODILES, AND BIRDS, KNOWN AS *DIAPSIDS*. (INCIDENTALLY, MAMMALS EVOLVED FROM A SEPARATE GROUP KNOWN AS *SYNAPSIDS*. THUS, DINOSAURS ARE NOT OUR ANCESTORS.)

ON THE GEOLOGICAL TIMESCALE, THE MESOZOIC ERA INCLUDES--FROM EARLIEST TO LATEST--THE TRIASSIC, JURASSIC, AND CRETACEOUS PERIODS. THE EARLIEST DINOSAURS APPEARED IN THE FORM OF ERECT-WALKING BIPEDS DURING THE MIDDLE TRIASSIC. SO WHAT KIND OF TIME PERIOD *WAS* THE TRIASSIC? GEOLOGICAL TIME SCALES ARE TYPICALLY MARKED BY SPECIES EXTINCTIONS BROUGHT ON BY SHIFTS IN THE ENVIRONMENT. AT THE END OF THE PERMIAN PERIOD, WHICH PRECEDED THE TRIASSIC, OVER 80% OF THE EARTH'S SPECIES WERE WIPED OUT, MARKING ONE OF THE MOST TREMENDOUS CATACLYSMS IN THE HISTORY OF THE WORLD. WITH A SURPLUS OF NEWLY OPENED ECOLOGICAL NICHES TO BE FILLED, DINOSAURS MADE THEIR ENTRANCE. HOWEVER, THESE NEWLY EMERGED DINOSAURS DID NOT INHERIT A POSITION OF DOMINANCE AMONGST LARGE ORGANISMS; RATHER, THAT SEAT WENT TO THE RELATIVES OF CROCODILES.

POSTOSUCHUS

A CROCODILIAN FROM THE MIDDLE AND LATE TRIASSIC WHICH COULD GROW UP TO FIVE METERS IN LENGTH. IT IS THOUGHT TO HAVE BEEN AN APEX PREDATOR IN ITS TIME.

EORAPTOR

ONE OF THE EARLIEST AND MOST PRIMITIVE DINOSAURS, THIS DINOSAUR FROM THE LATE TRIASSIC GREW TO ABOUT ONE METER IN LENGTH. THE EORAPTOR BORE CHARACTERISTICS OF BOTH THE THEROPODA AND SAUROPODA SUBORDERS, MAKING ITS CORRECT CLASSIFICATION A SUBJECT OF DEBATE.

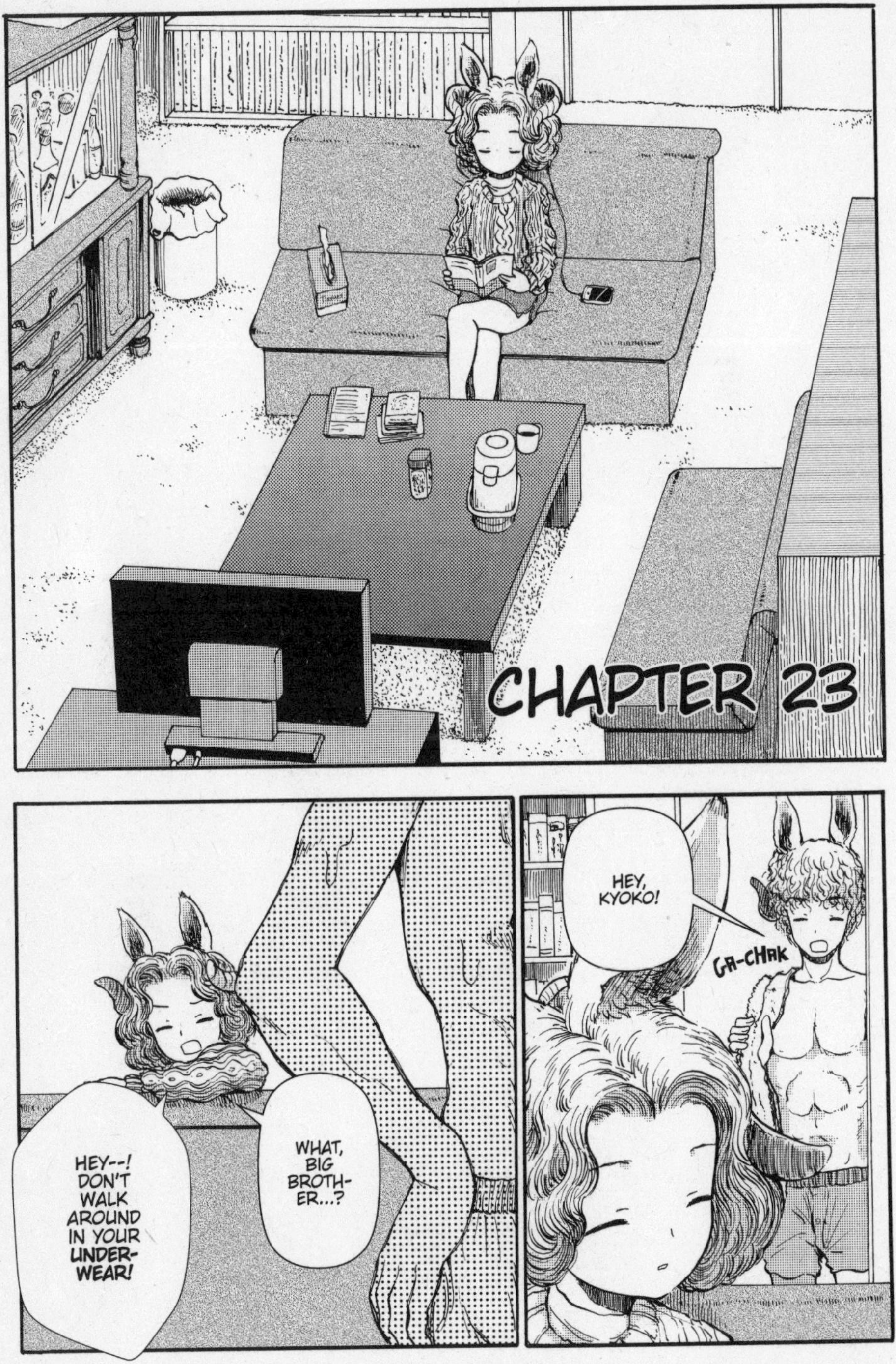
CHAPTER 23
HEY, KYOKO!
GA-CHAK
WHAT, BIG BROTHER...?
HEY--! DON'T WALK AROUND IN YOUR UNDERWEAR!

WHAT'S THE BIG DEAL WHEN I'M INSIDE?
DAD DOES IT ALL THE TIME.
So hot...
YOU'RE BOTH CRUDE.
YOU SHOULD BE MORE CAREFUL WITH AN ADOLESCENT GIRL AROUND THE HOUSE.
AN ADOLES-CENT GIRL, HUH?
WHERE?
OKAY, OKAY--!

SO, WHAT DO YOU WANT?
WELL, SINCE YOU'RE IN CHARGE OF LUNCH TOMORROW AND I HAVE A PRACTICE MATCH, CAN YOU MAKE ME A PACKED LUNCH?
WHAT?!
JUST BUY SOMETHING FROM THE CONVENIENCE STORE.
I DON'T LIKE EATING OUT. EVERYTHING IS EITHER TOO SALTY OR TOO SWEET.
THEN FIX SOME-THING.
I'M ALREADY HEADING TO BED.
I have to wake up really early.
WAIT, SO YOU WANT *ME* TO WAKE UP EVEN EARLIER FOR YOU?
OR YOU CAN MAKE IT TONIGHT.
AND SINCE I'M DOING SPORTS, THINK ABOUT THE NUTRITION I NEED.
ARE YOU KIDDING ME?!

SO... YOU MADE IT FOR HIM?
IT WAS THE ONLY WAY TO SHUT HIM UP.
EEP, A SNAKE-FOLK!
OUR STORE DOESN'T CARRY ANY ITEMS FOR SNAKEFOLK... WILL WE BE REPORTED?!

That was a snakefolk just now.
They really exist.
Phew...
Time to eat!
Yeah!
I'm starving!
Doesn't this place have a microwave?
NARAKU, IS THAT A HOMEMADE LUNCH?
YEAH.
YOU LUCKY, BASTARD!

I'M SO SICK OF THOSE WEIRD LUNCHES AT CONVENIENCE STORES.
TELL ME ABOUT IT, I'M TIRED OF MY *MOM'S* LUNCHES.
ISN'T HIS LUNCH MADE BY HIS LITTLE SISTER?
NO WAY!
I'M SO JEALOUS. OLDER SISTERS ARE THE WORST.
I'M JEALOUS EITHER WAY.
IT SUCKS TO BE SURROUNDED BY BOYS BOTH AT HOME *AND* SCHOOL.
YOU GUYS HAVE TOO MUCH IMAGINATION, THAT'S NOT HOW IT IS.
UNDER-STANDABLE WITH A **FACE** LIKE YOURS.
WHAT THE HELL, MAN?! WHAT ARE YOU TRYING TO SAY?! I'LL KILL YOU!
DO IT IF YOU CAN, YOU LOUSY PITCHER!
WH-WHAT DID YOU SAY?!
SHUT UP!

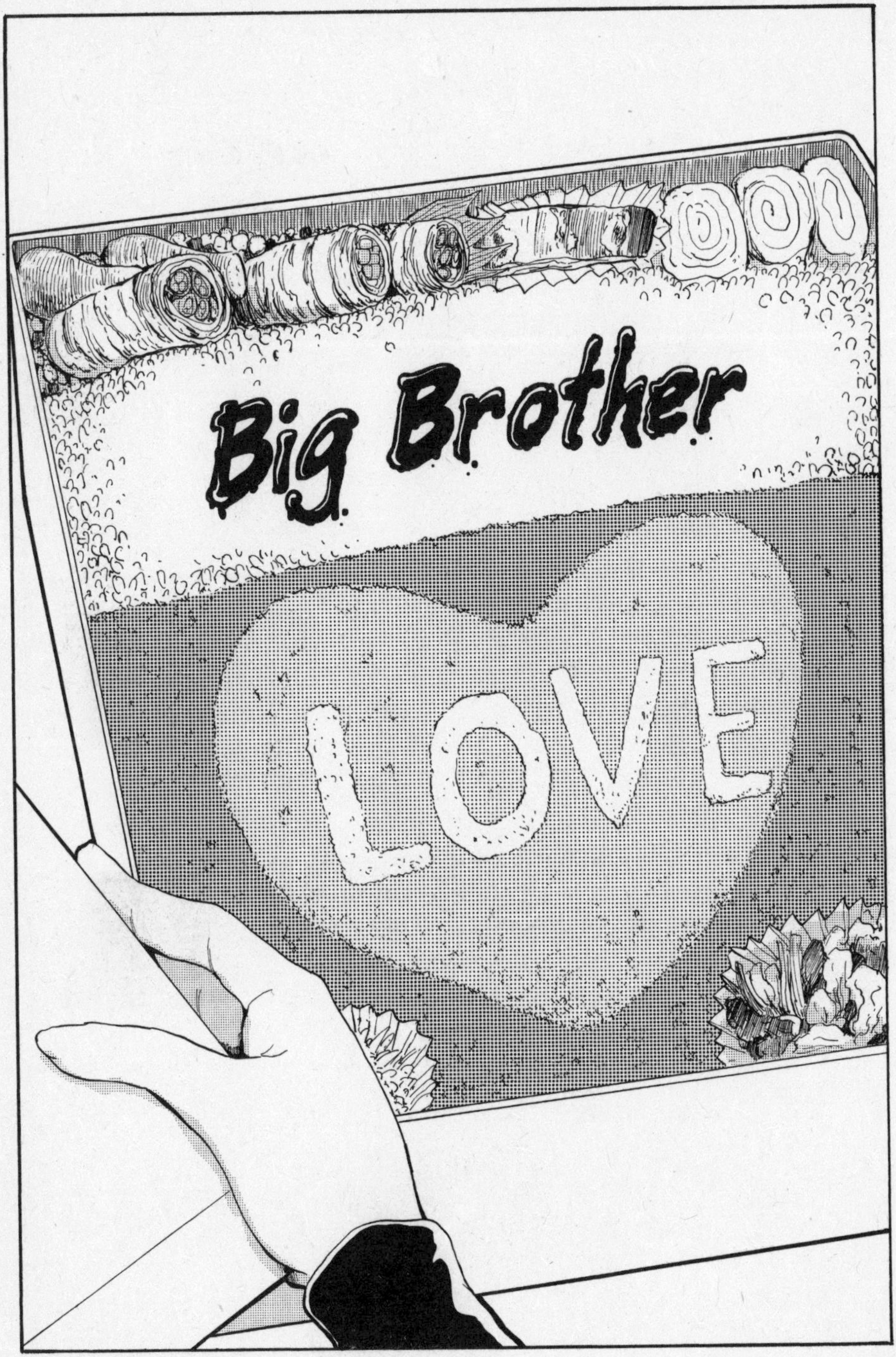
Big Brother
LOVE

WHAT? YOU'RE SO NOISY.	KYOKO!

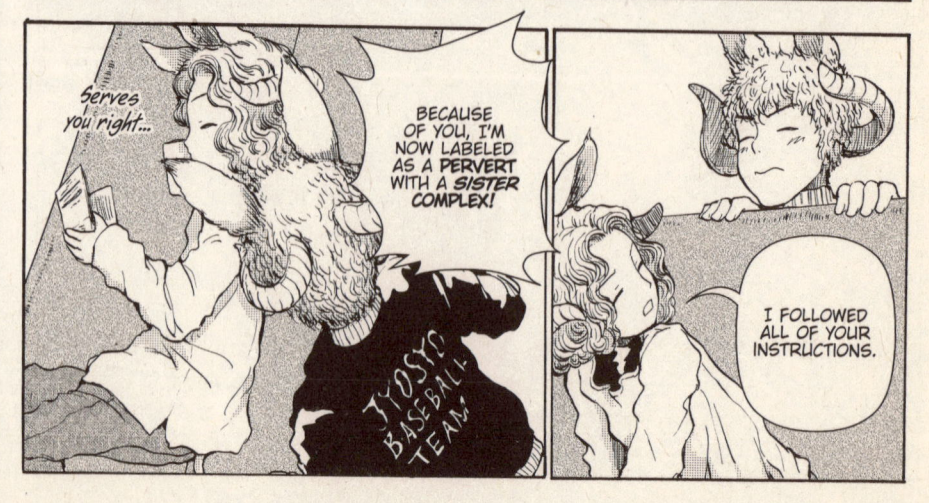

WHAT DID YOU DO TO MY LUNCH!

Hey, Naraku's lunch is amazing!

Serves you right...

BECAUSE OF YOU, I'M NOW LABELED AS A PERVERT WITH A SISTER COMPLEX!

I FOLLOWED ALL OF YOUR INSTRUCTIONS.

JYOSYO BASEBALL TEAM

Fine, fine!

IT WAS THE ONLY WAY TO SHUT HIM UP.

AS AN APOLOGY, HE TOLD ME TO BRING MY FRIENDS TO CHEER FOR THEIR GAME AGAINST KAISEI.

SO, WHY ARE WE GOING TO CHEER FOR KYOKO'S BROTHER?

KAISEI IS GOOD... THEY WENT TO THE HIGH SCHOOL BASEBALL INVITATIONAL.

CAN YOUR BROTHER'S TEAM BEAT THEM?

THEY'RE BOTH SCHOOLS FULL OF BASEBALL IDIOTS, BUT MY BROTHER'S SCHOOL RANKED LOWER.

It's where people go when they can't get into Kaisei.

National High School Baseball
← Big Brother's School

I DON'T REALLY GET IT EITHER.

I DON'T UNDER-STAND.

JUST HAVING GIRLS COME CHEER FOR THEM IS A WIN.

ACCORDING TO MY BROTHER...

LET'S DO THIS!

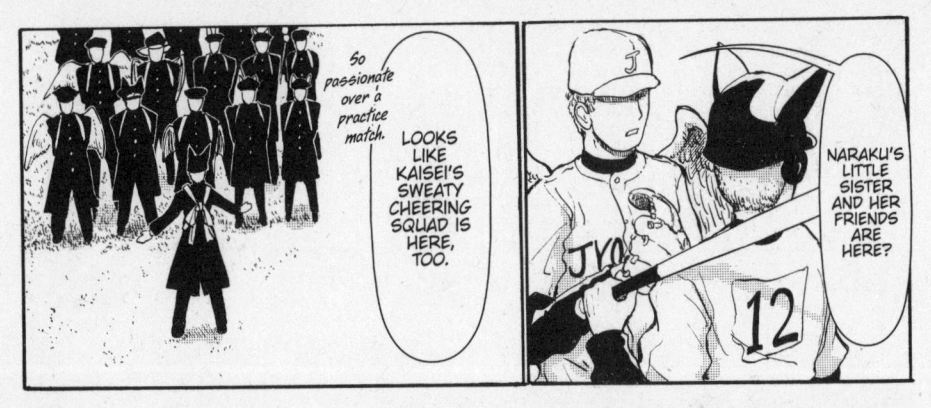

So passionate over a practice match.

Looks like Kaisei's sweaty cheering squad is here, too.

Naraku's little sister and her friends are here?

The one on the far left must be Naraku's sister.

You can tell just by looking.

Check it out.

This is the first time I've watched a real baseball game. So exciting!

It's pretty much the same as softball.

Whoa... her friends are all pretty hot.

Naraku better not be dating any of them.

What about that one?

Um... is it racist to say she's not my type?

※ Kaisei's Bench
HEY, LOOK AT THAT.
THERE ARE GIRLS HERE.
NO WAY. THEY MUST BE LOST OR SOMETHING.
You can do it!
Come on, Jyosyo!
All right, Jyosyo!
Beat Kaisei!
THEY'RE CHEERING FOR JYOSYO?!
WHAT?! WE'RE THE BETTER TEAM!
THEY'RE WEAK BECAUSE THEY WASTE TIME ON GIRLS!
YEAH! UH-HUH!

THAT'S ENOUGH! EVERYONE CALM DOWN!
YES, COACH!
THOSE GIRLS ARE PRETTY CUTE, HUH?
Which one?
Hey, there's Kyoko's big bro!
DO YOU ALL WANT GIRLFRIENDS LIKE THAT?
YES, SIR!
THEN GET OUT THERE AND DOMINATE!
THOSE GIRLS WILL BE LOOKING AT YOU INSTEAD!
KEEP WINNING, AND YOU'LL BE ABLE TO GET GIRLS, FAME, AND MONEY! GOT IT?!
YES, SIR!

HIMENO-SAN...?

KAISEI'S PITCHER... ISN'T HE THE GUY WHO GAVE YOU THAT LOVE LETTER?

HE WAS A RELIEF PITCHER LAST SUMMER. HE'S REALLY GOOD, THOUGH.

HE MIGHT BE KAISEI'S NEXT ACE PITCHER.

PLAY BALL!

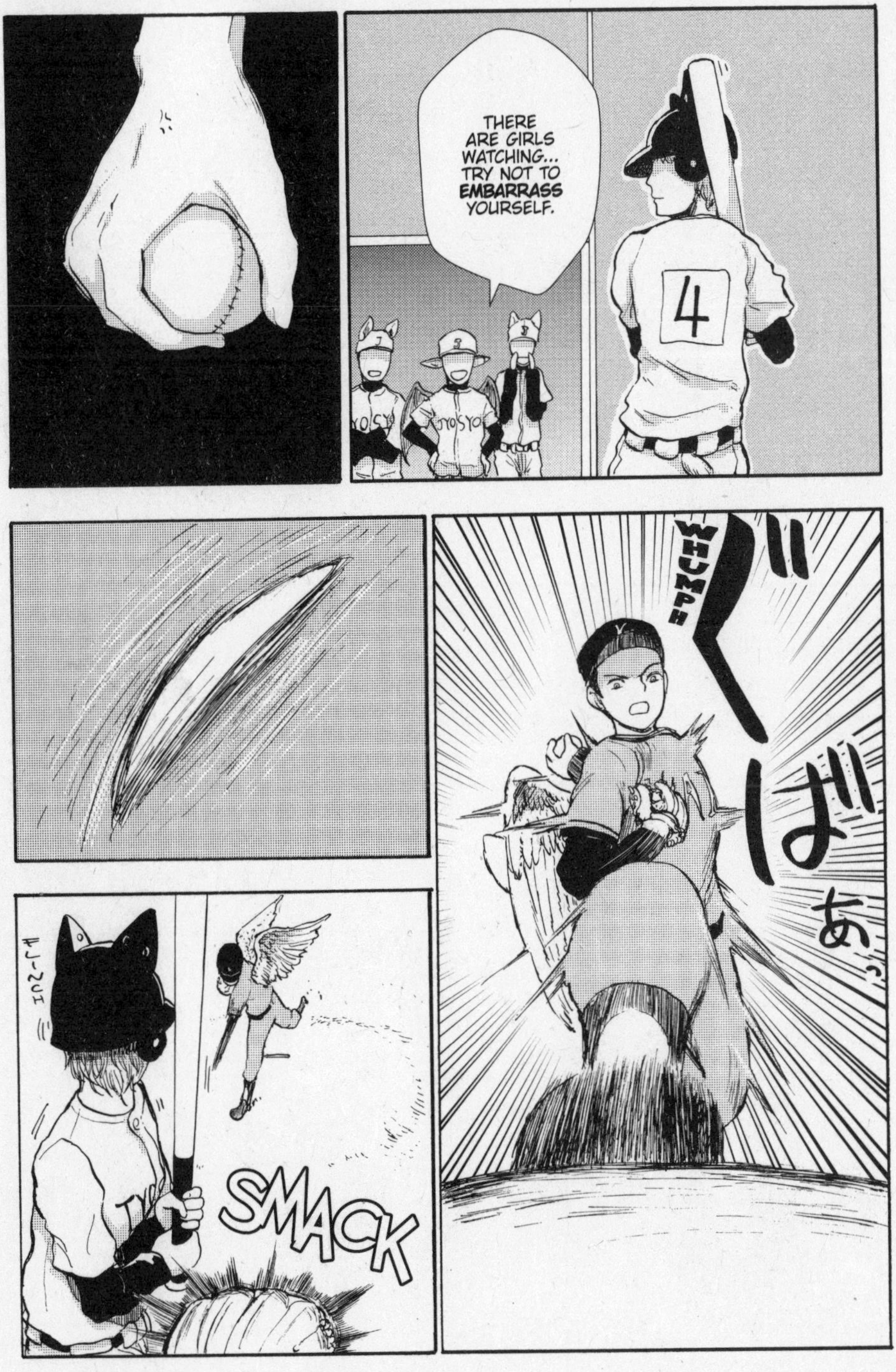
THERE ARE GIRLS WATCHING... TRY NOT TO EMBARRASS YOURSELF.
WHUMPH
ばぁっ
SMACK

NICE PITCH!
HEY, NOW ...!
WOW. HIS PITCH IS REALLY FAST.
How fast? Any idea?
About 150 kph.
STRIKE! BATTER OUT!
1
2
Jyosyo
0
Kaisei
DON'T WORRY. IT'S JUST THE FIRST INNING.
JYOSY
LET'S DO THIS!

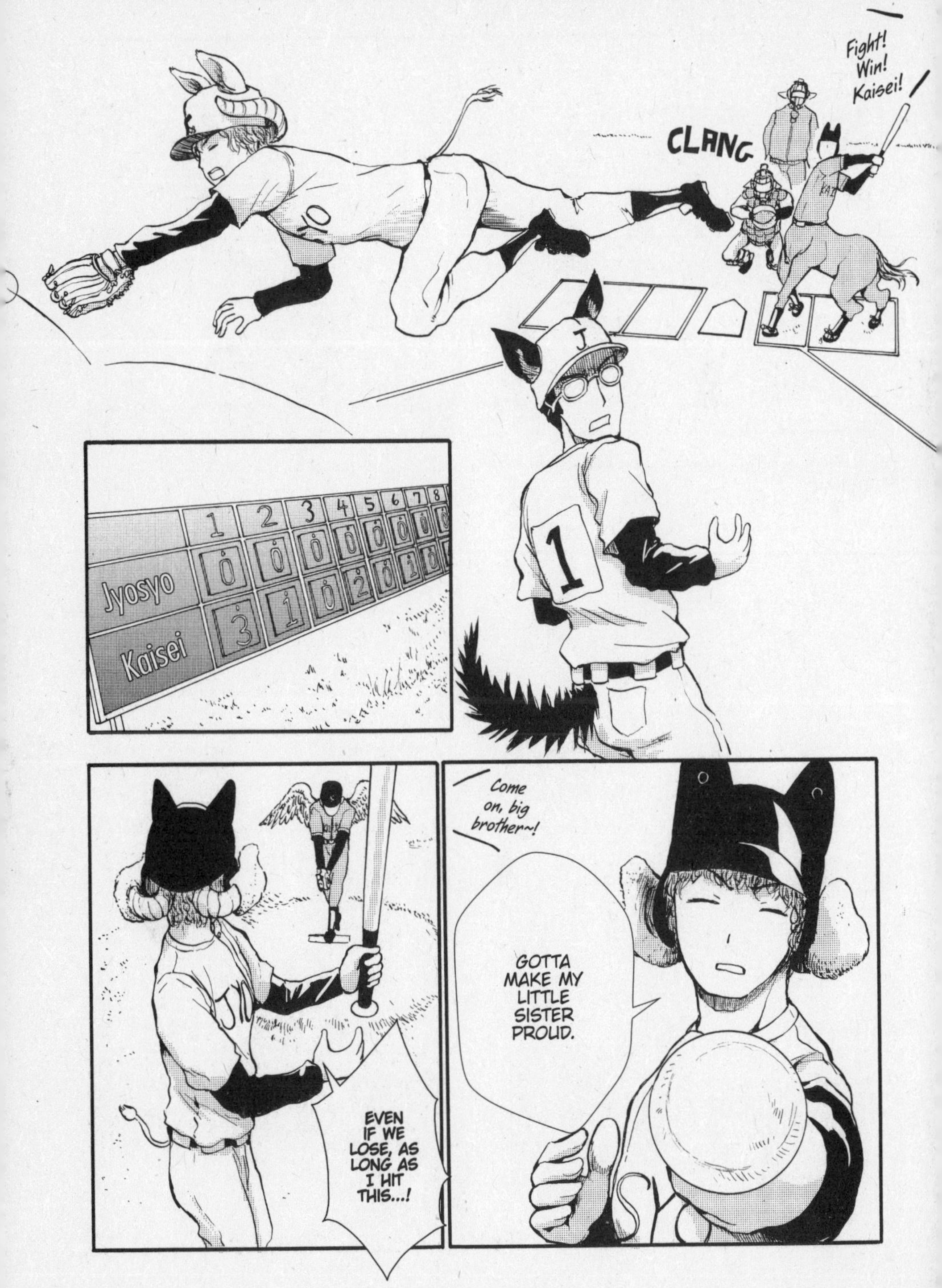
CLANG
Fight! Win! Kaisei!
1 2 3 4 5 6 7 8
Jyosyo
Kaisei
Come on, big brother~!
GOTTA MAKE MY LITTLE SISTER PROUD.
EVEN IF WE LOSE, AS LONG AS I HIT THIS...!

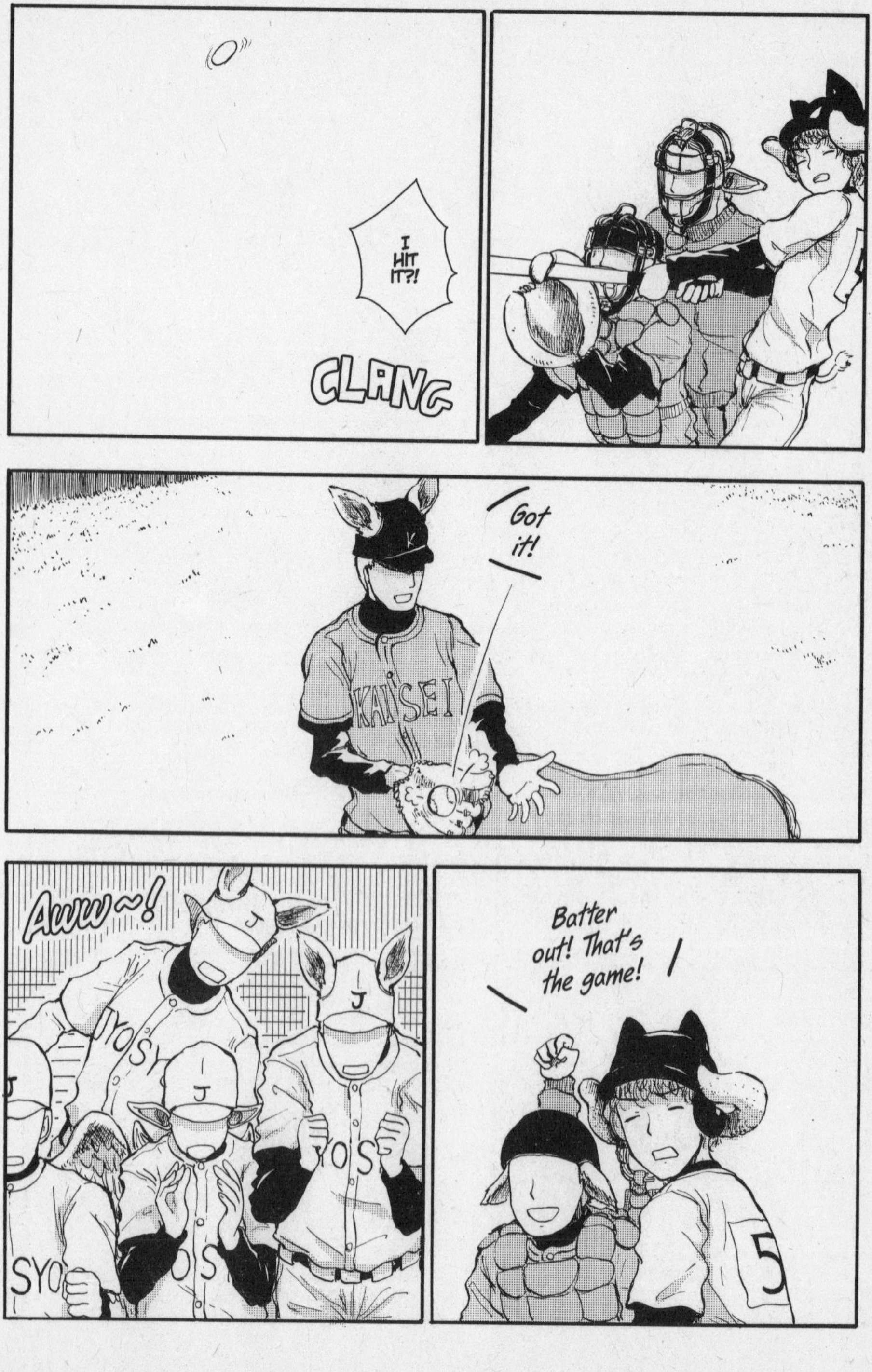
I HIT IT?!
CLANG
Got it!
Aww~!
Batter out! That's the game!

THEY LOST.

NOT SURPRISING.

Good game.
Good game.
Good game.

YEAH... IT'S HARD TO FIND THE RIGHT WORDS FOR THE LOSING TEAM.

WELL, LET'S GO HOME.

I'll treat you all to cocoa.

YOU KNOW WE DON'T GET FREE TIME AFTER GAMES, STUPID!

ALL RIGHT. TIME TO HIT ON THOSE GIRLS.

KA-CHAK
TAP TAP TAP
WELCOME HOME, BIG BROTHER.
SILENCE
?
YOSYO
ASEBALL
TEAM

SORRY.
YOU AND YOUR FRIENDS DIDN'T SEE MY COOL SIDE.
JYOSYO BASEBALL TEAM
DON'T WORRY, WE WEREN'T EXPECTING MUCH.
Now he's pouting...
JYOSYO BASEBALL TEAM
LOOK, THERE WAS NOTHING YOU COULD DO. THEY WERE JUST THE BETTER TEAM.
I'M NOT SMART LIKE YOU.
THE ONLY THING I HAVE GOING FOR ME IS **BASEBALL.**

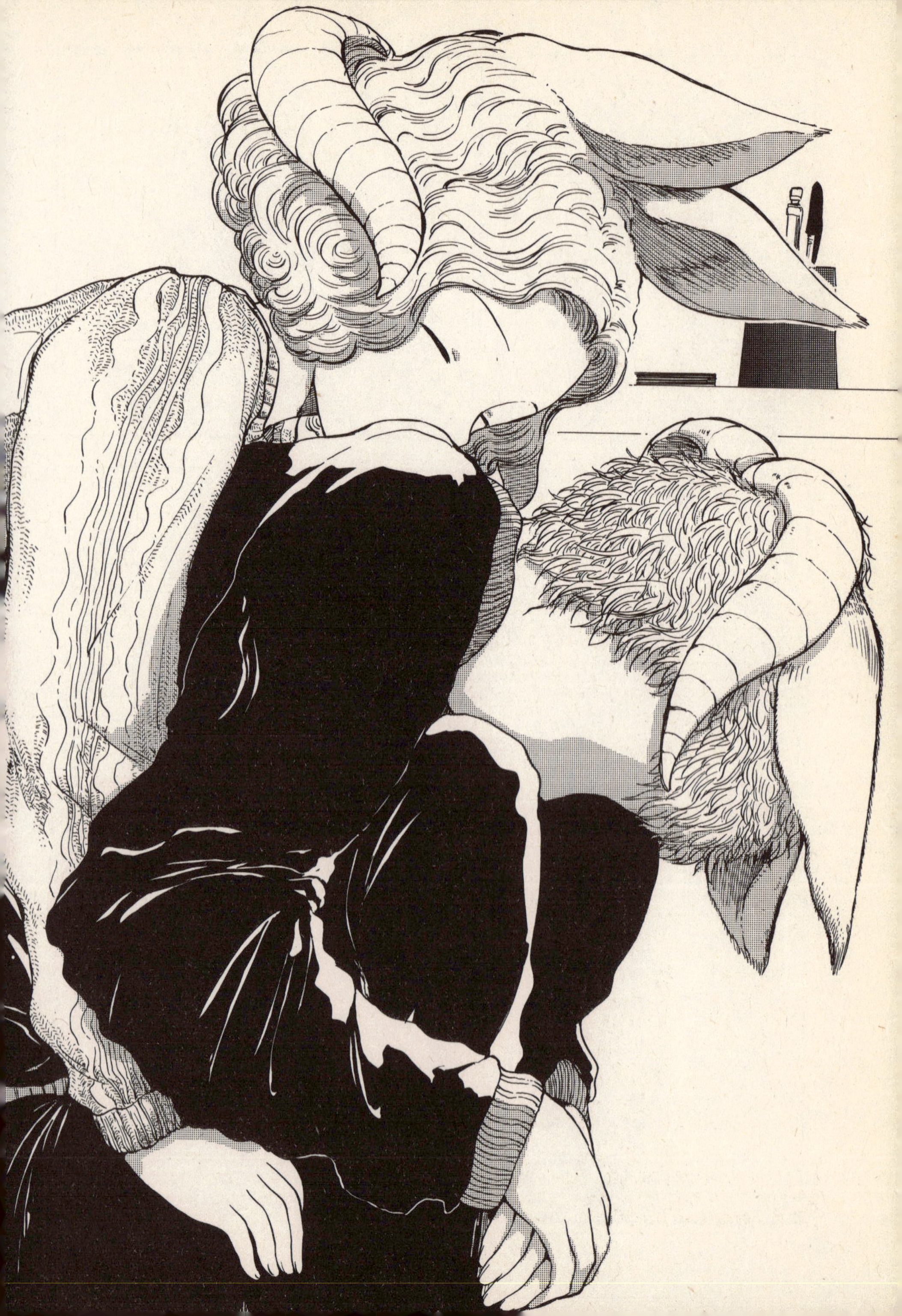

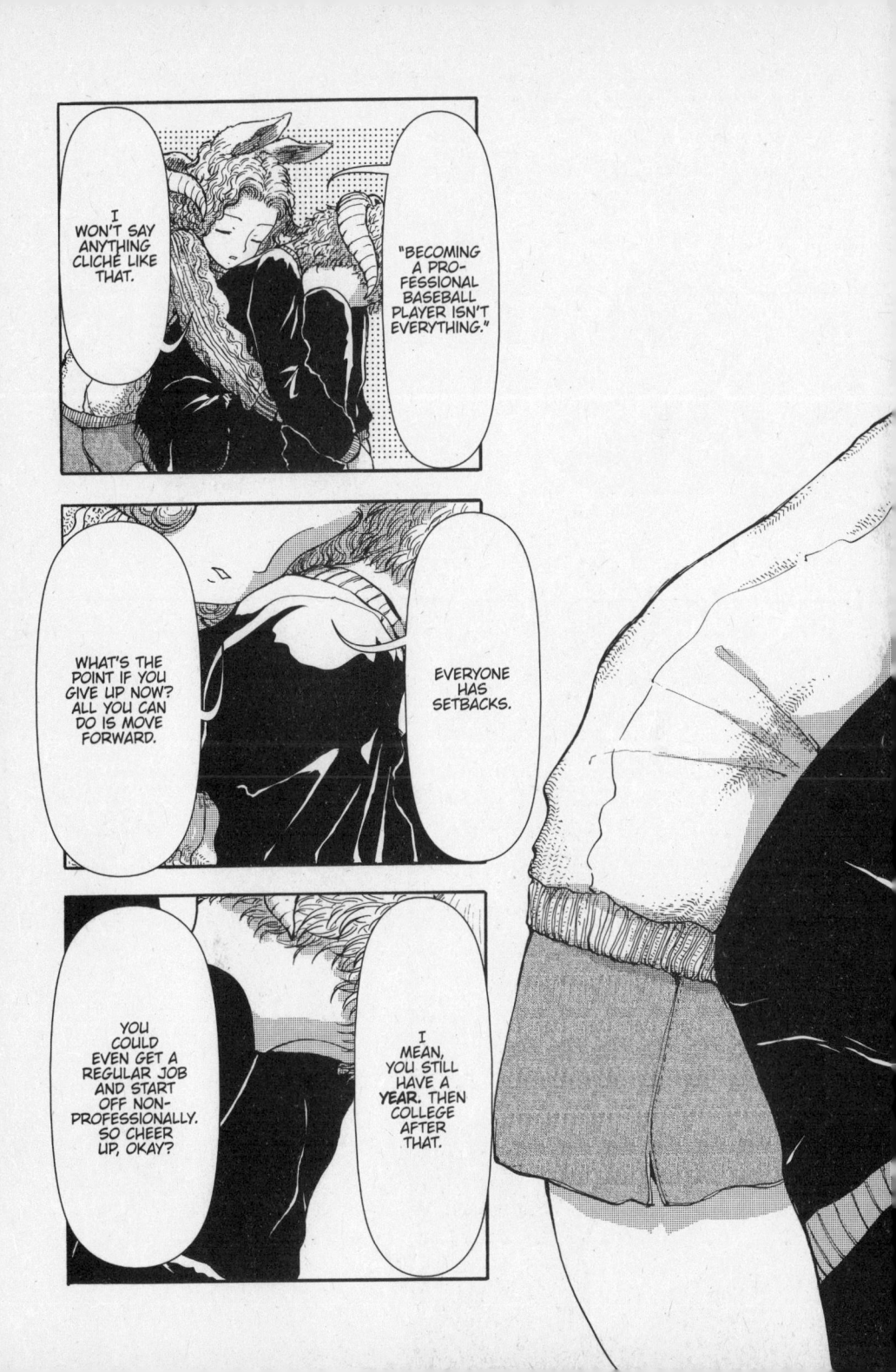

| I WON'T SAY ANYTHING CLICHE LIKE THAT. | "BECOMING A PRO-FESSIONAL BASEBALL PLAYER ISN'T EVERYTHING." |

| WHAT'S THE POINT IF YOU GIVE UP NOW? ALL YOU CAN DO IS MOVE FORWARD. | EVERYONE HAS SETBACKS. |

| YOU COULD EVEN GET A REGULAR JOB AND START OFF NON-PROFESSIONALLY. SO CHEER UP, OKAY? | I MEAN, YOU STILL HAVE A YEAR. THEN COLLEGE AFTER THAT. |

YOU'RE REALLY FLAT-CHESTED.

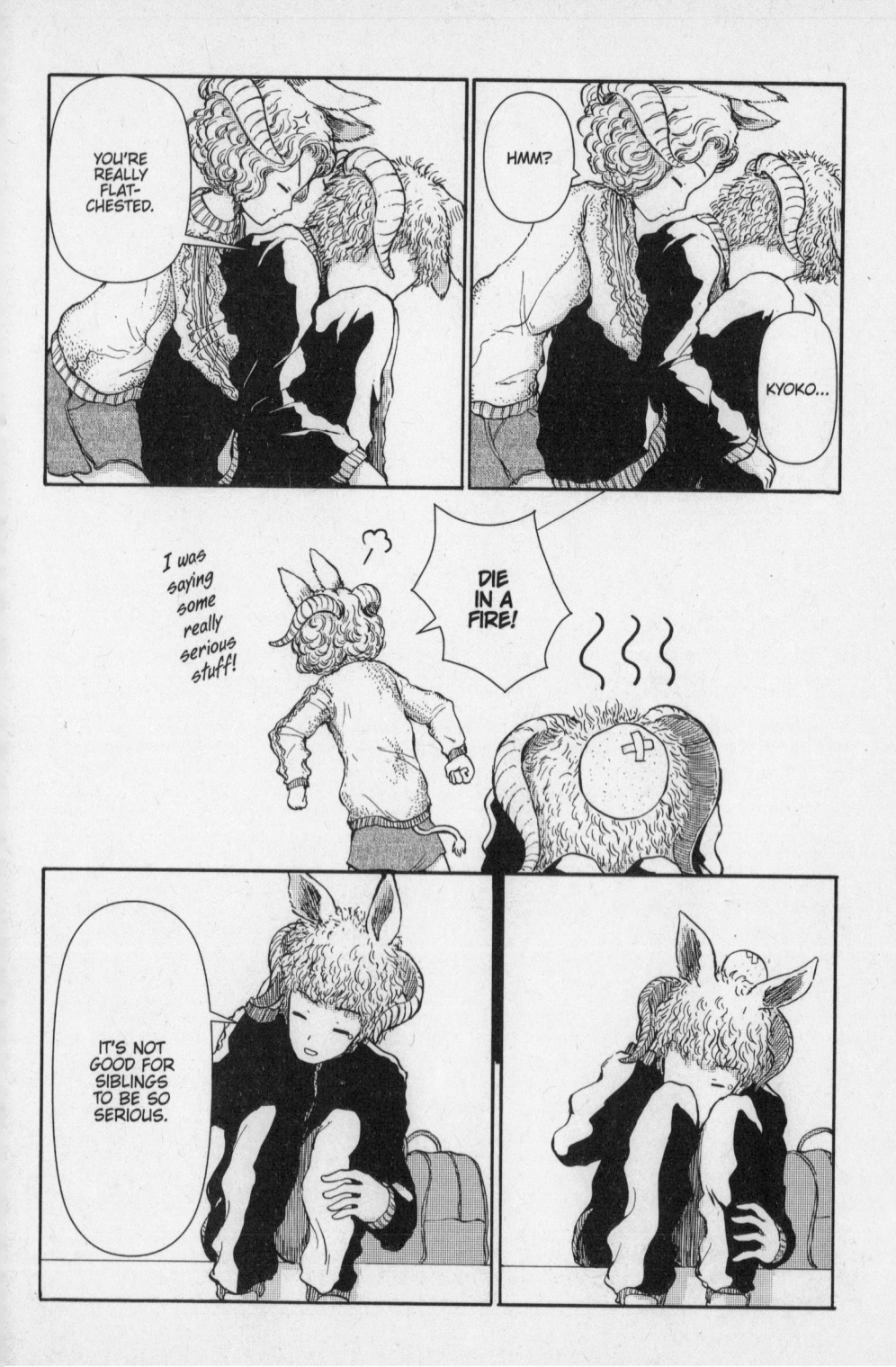

HMM?

KYOKO...

I was saying some really serious stuff!

DIE IN A FIRE!

IT'S NOT GOOD FOR SIBLINGS TO BE SO SERIOUS.

A Centaur's Life

MESOZOIC CREATURES

DINOSAURS AND THEIR CLOSE RELATIVES: ON THE PROGRESSION OF DINOSAURS AND THEIR AIR SAC SYSTEM

THE WORLD DURING THE TRIASSIC PERIOD WAS ONE OF INTENSE HEAT AND LOW OXYGEN. DURING THE PALEOZOIC ERA, THE EARTH'S OXYGEN CONCENTRATION REACHED A HEIGHT OF 35%, DROPPING ALL THE WAY DOWN TO 10% BY THE END OF THE TRIASSIC (IN MODERN TIMES, IT IS AT APPROXIMATELY 20%).

AS SUCH, THE CLOSING OF THE TRIASSIC PERIOD BROUGHT WITH IT ANOTHER MASS EXTINCTION. DINOSAURS MANAGED TO SURVIVE, AND AS THE EARTH'S OXYGEN LEVEL GRADUALLY INCREASED IN THE SUBSEQUENT JURASSIC AND CRETACEOUS PERIODS, THEY ACTUALLY INCREASED IN DIVERSITY AND SECURED THEIR POSITION OF DOMINANCE. BUT WHAT ALLOWED THEM TO DO THIS?

DINOSAURS ARE BELIEVED TO HAVE HAD A RESPIRATORY ORGAN CALLED AN *AIR SAC*, MUCH LIKE THAT OF MODERN BIRDS (OR MORE ACCURATELY, BIRDS *INHERITED* THIS AIR SAC FEATURE FROM DINOSAURS). IN CONTRAST TO THE TWO-WAY BREATHING METHOD OF MAMMALS, WHERE THE EXPANSION AND CONTRACTION OF THE THORAX AND DIAPHRAGM FILLS AND EMPTIES THE LUNGS, THE AIR SAC SYSTEM IS MORE EFFICIENT. THE AIR ENTERS THE AIR SAC, PASSES THROUGH THE LUNGS AND THEN FLOWS INTO *ANOTHER* AIR SAC, WHICH FINALLY EXPELS THE AIR. THE EXISTENCE OF THIS EFFICIENT RESPIRATORY SYSTEM IS WHAT ALLOWS BIRDS TO GENERATE THE VAST AMOUNTS OF ENERGY NEEDED TO BEAT THEIR WINGS AND STAY ALOFT. IT IS THIS VERY SAME METHOD THAT ALLOWED THE DINOSAURS TO ENDURE A LOW-OXYGEN AGE, PUSH THEIR WAY PAST OTHER SPECIES, AND PROGRESS AS A GROUP.

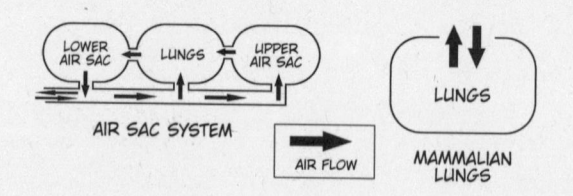

OVIRAPTOR

A THEROPOD TWO TO THREE METERS IN LENGTH THAT THRIVED DURING THE LATE CRETACEOUS PERIOD. DUE TO AN EARLY FOSSIL DISCOVERY IN WHICH THE OVIRAPTOR WAS FOUND OVERLAIN WITH A PILE OF EGGS, IT WAS GIVEN THE NICKNAME "EGG TAKER," BUT FURTHER RESEARCH REVEALED THAT THE DINOSAUR WAS IN FACT PROTECTING ITS OWN EGGS. HOWEVER, THE RAPTOR'S TOOTHLESS BEAK AND UPPER BONE STRUCTURE RESEMBLE THAT OF THE EGG-EATING SNAKE, SUGGESTING IT MAY HAVE BEEN AN EGG-EATER NONETHELESS.

Weee!
POUNCE
Good morning.
Good morning, teacher.
DASH
MAKI-CHAN, GOOD MORNING!

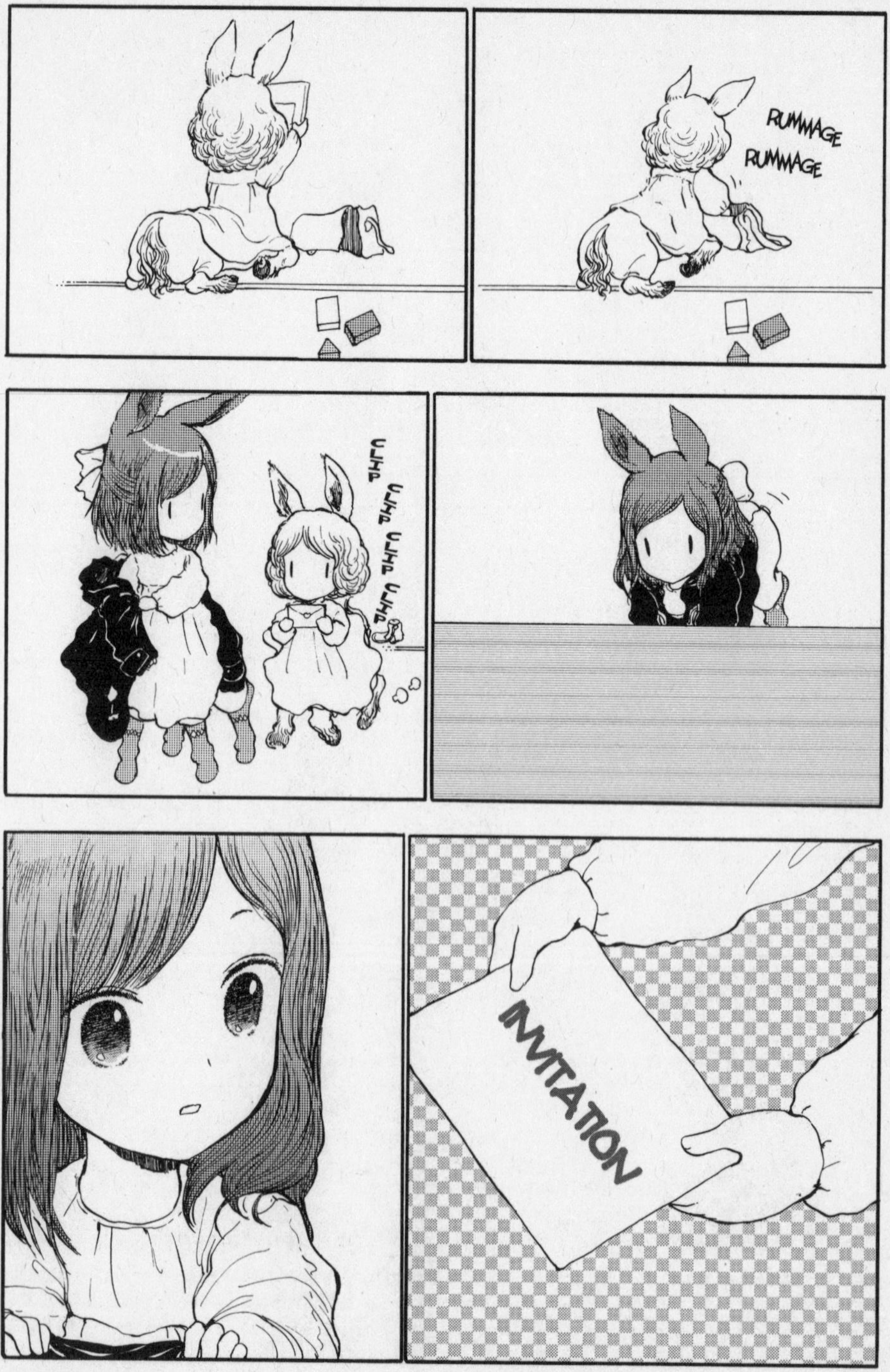
RUMMAGE
RUMMAGE
CLIP CLIP CLIP CLIP
INVITATION

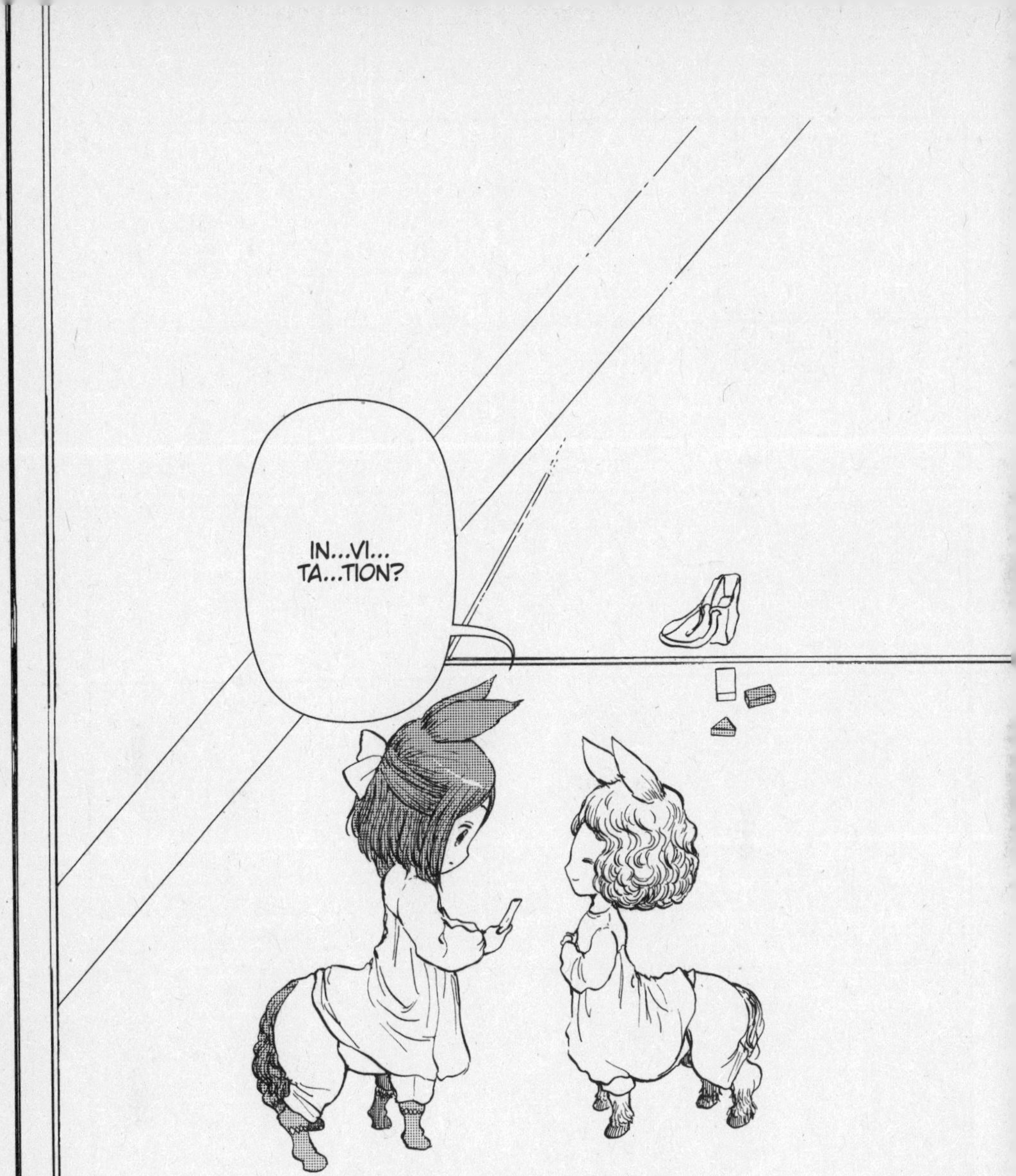
IN...VI... TA...TION?

CHAPTER 24

DID YOU WRITE THIS MAKI-CHAN? GOOD JOB!
YEAH.
Big Sister Shino-chan
Merry Xmas
Christmas Party
CHRISTMAS PARTY?
YEAH.
WHO ELSE IS GOING?
JUST BIG SIS SHINO-CHAN!
YOU'RE NOT GOING TO INVITE TA-CHAN?
NOT... OKAY?
IT'S FINE, BUT...

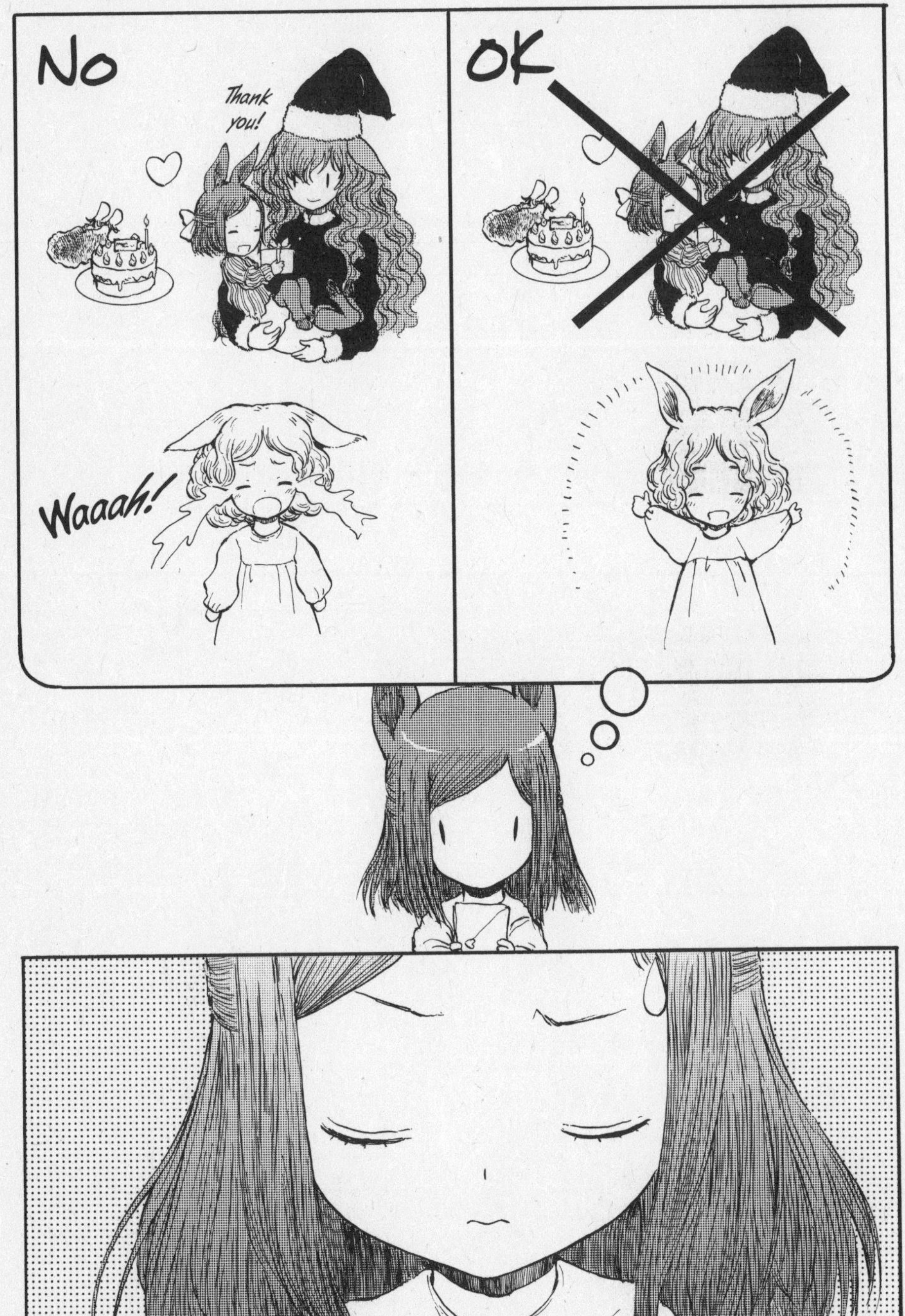
No
Thank you!
Waaah!
OK

YAY!

I'LL ASK MY MOM IF I CAN GO.

STUFF STUFF

I THINK YOU SHOULD GO TO MAKI-CHAN'S.
HUH?
BUT... DOESN'T BIG SISTER WANT TO BE WITH SHINO FOR CHRISTMAS?
OF COURSE BIG SISTER WANTS TO SPEND CHRISTMAS WITH SHINO-CHAN.
BUT MAKI-CHAN IS SMALLER THAN SHINO-CHAN, RIGHT?
YOU SHOULD GRANT MAKI-CHAN'S WISH.
HOW COME?

BECAUSE CHRISTMAS IS THE DAY YOU DO SOMETHING SPECIAL...
...FOR SOMEONE SMALLER THAN YOURSELF.
We can spend next Christmas together.
Hee!
HIME-CHAN IS AMAZING.
She says good things.
CLUNK

Thank you very much for inviting us today.
This isn't much, but please take it.
Oh, my. Thank you.
Thank you for always taking care of our Maki-chan.
BIG SIS LOOKS LIKE A PWINCESS!
I'LL COME BACK TO PICK HER UP AROUND SEVEN.
So much food!
POFF
POFF
UM, THIS IS A PRESENT FOR YOU.

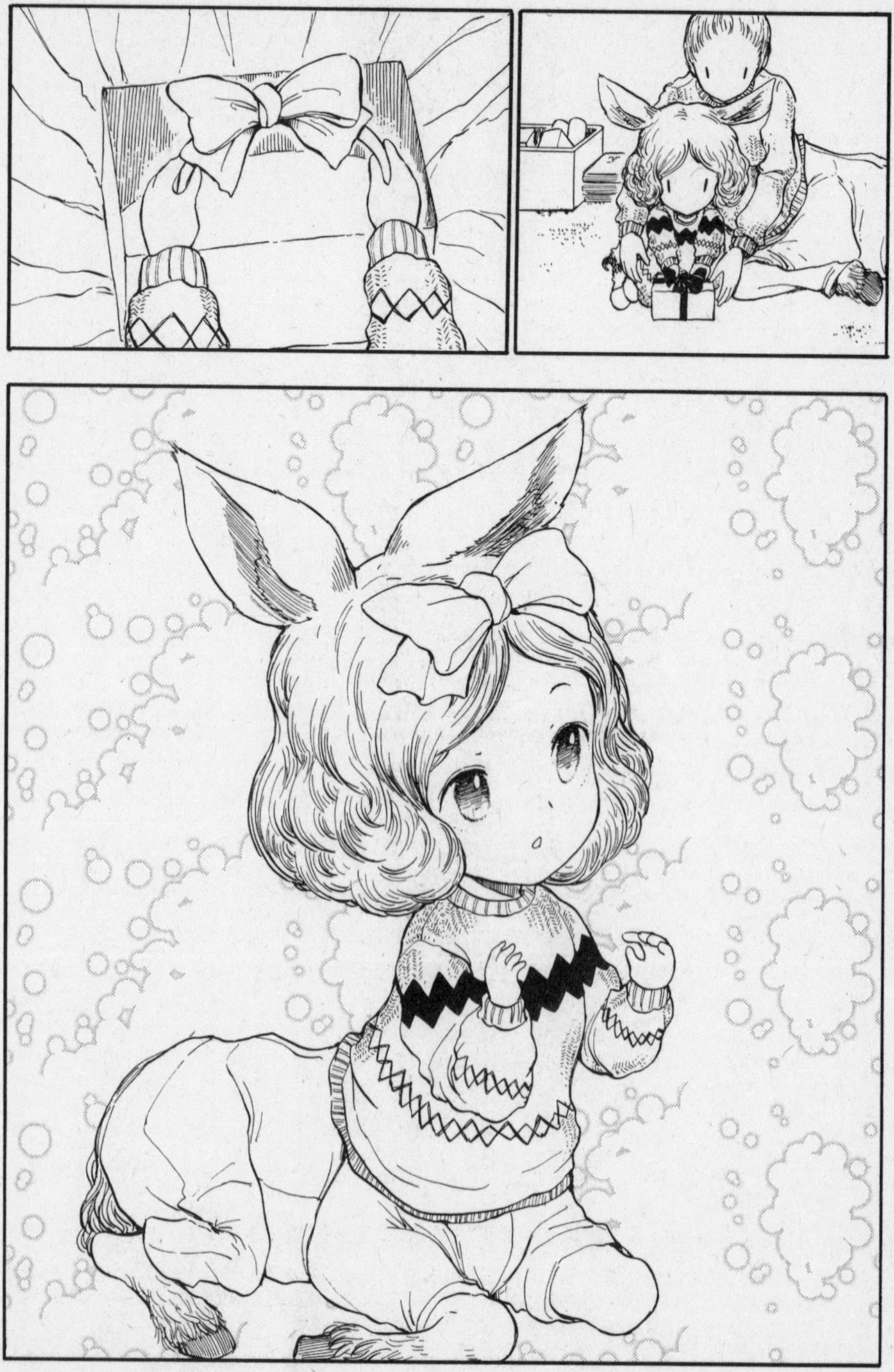

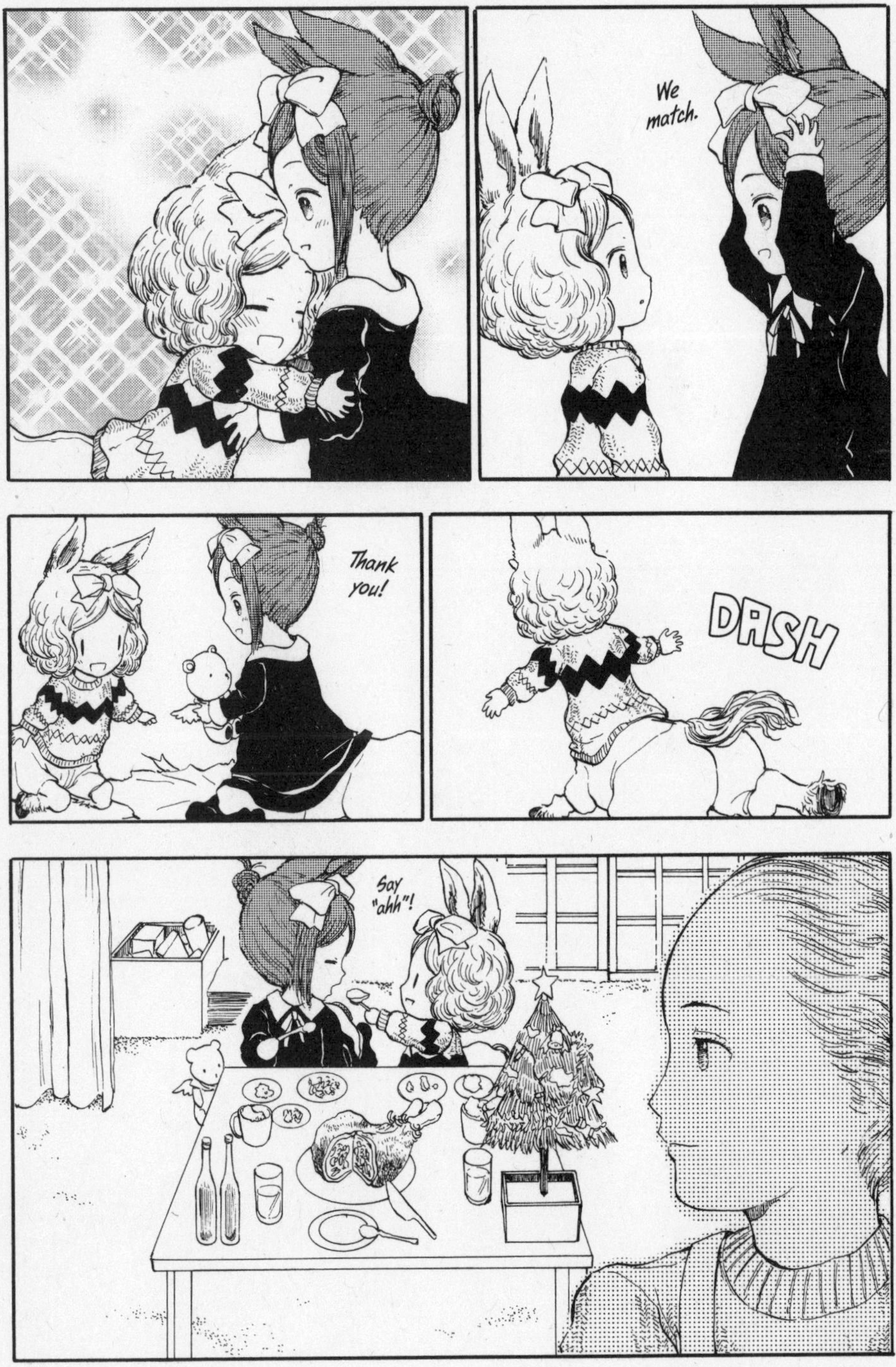
We match.
Thank you!
DASH
Say "ahh"!

Thank you very much for the food. / My, my... so polite!	IT WAS YUMMY! / I'M SO FULL.

THIS. / OKAY, LET'S WATCH! LET'S WATCH! / DESTINY ANIMATION — Snow White	BIG SIS, DO YOU WANNA WATCH PWINCESS? / Pwincess?

♪

IT LOOKS LIKE MAKI-CHAN IS A PWINCESS!
THE PWINCESS HAS A BOW TOO!

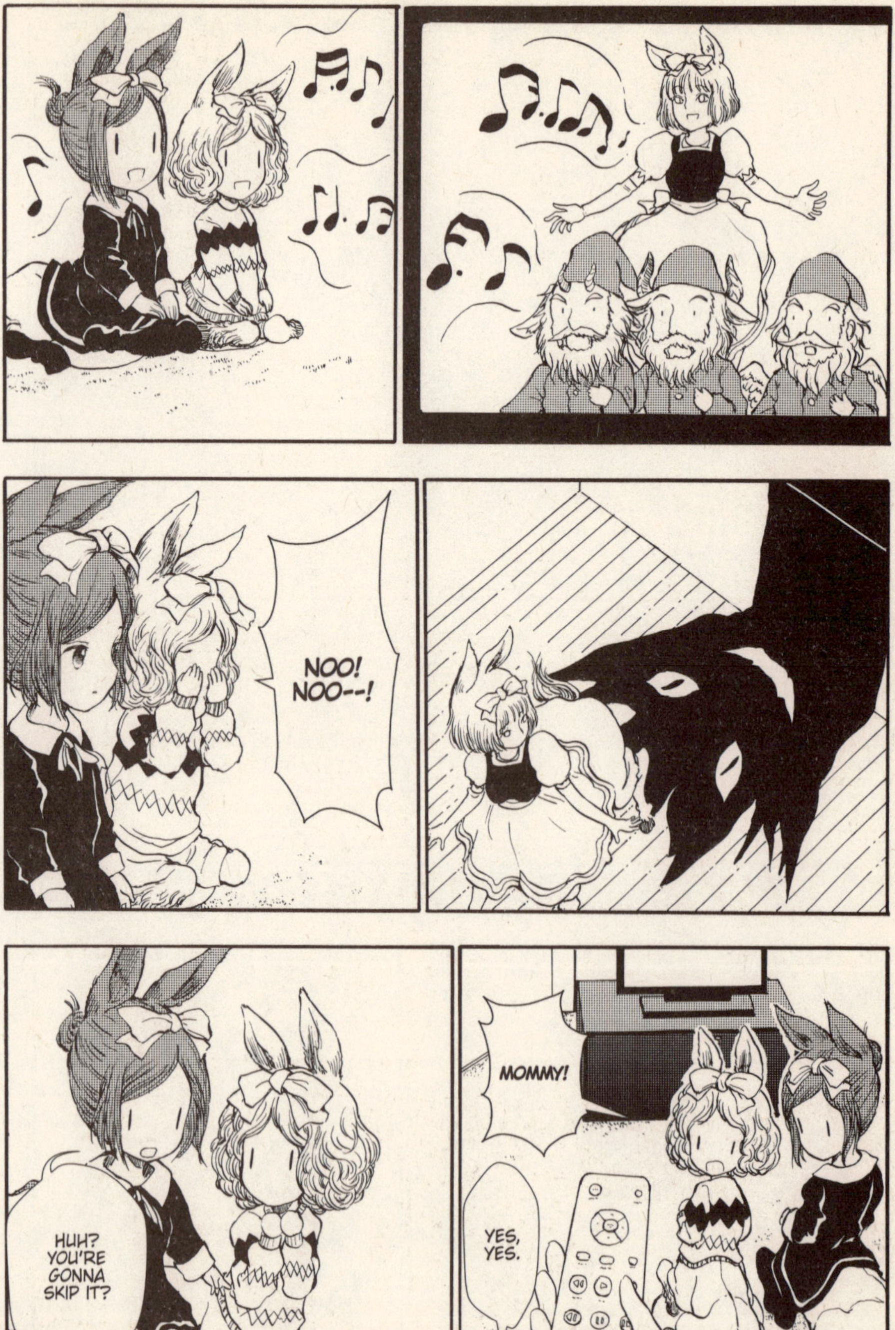
NOO! NOO--!
MOMMY!
YES, YES.
HUH? YOU'RE GONNA SKIP IT?

THE WITCH IS SCARY!
BUT IF YOU DON'T SEE THE WITCH, THE STORY GETS MESSED UP.
BIG SIS WANTS TO SEE IT ALL.
UMYUU~!
WHAT IF...

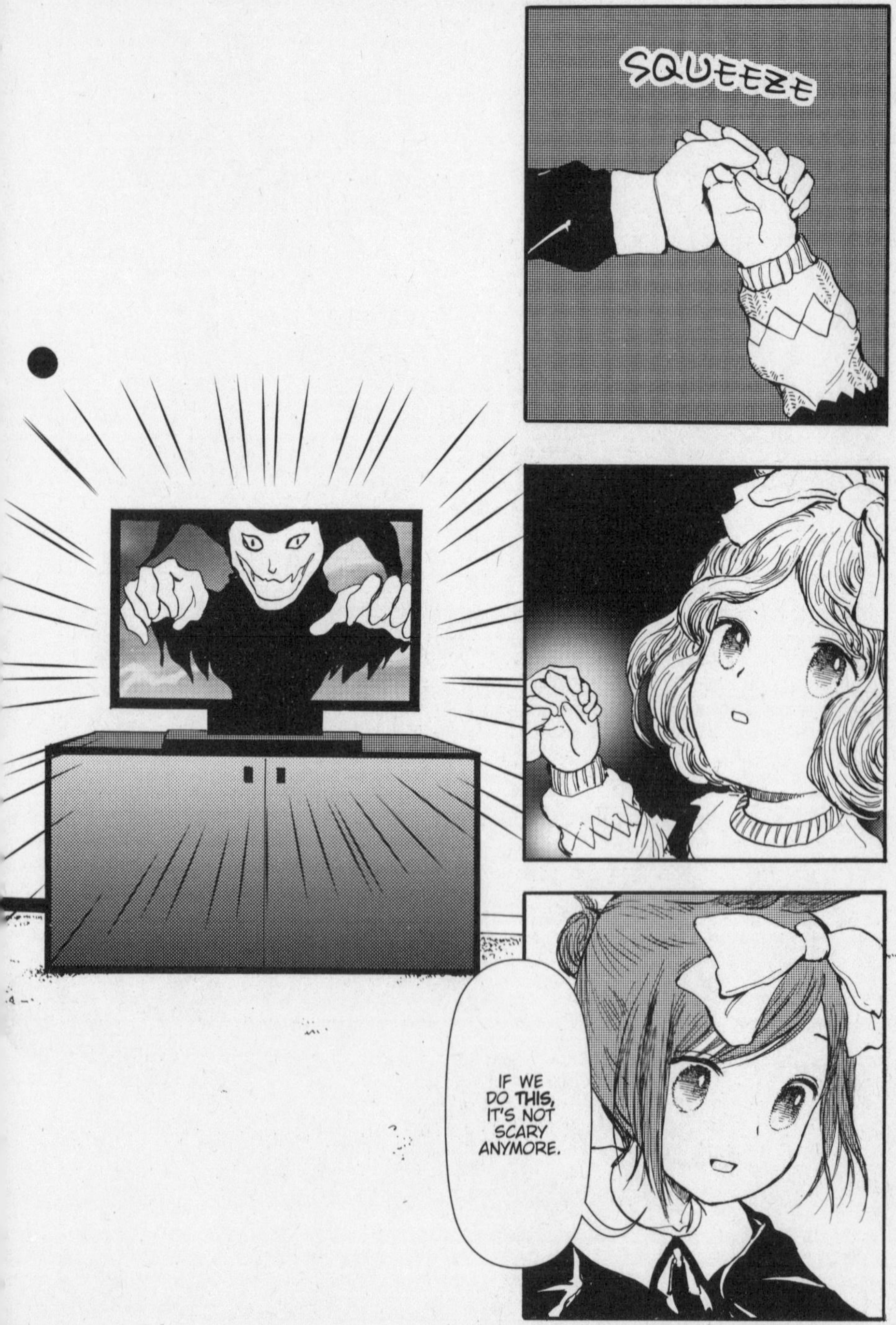
SQUEEZE
IF WE DO THIS, IT'S NOT SCARY ANYMORE.

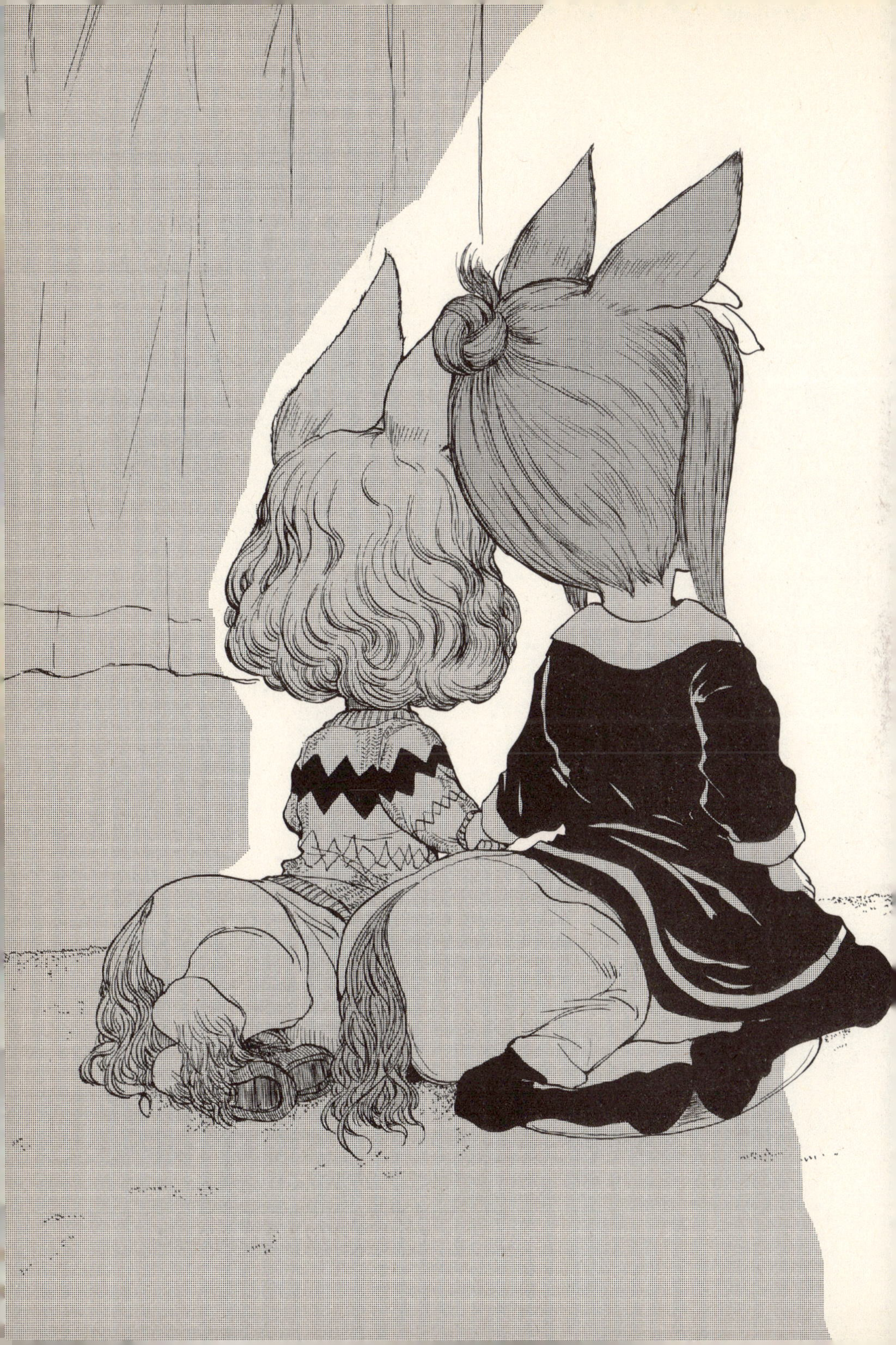

That was fun.

See you later!

Mommy!

VROOM

MAKI-CHAN, TAKE OFF YOUR BOW.
NO!
I'M GONNA WEAR IT FOR-EVER.
BUT YOU'RE GOING TO TAKE A BATH. IT'LL GET WET AND DIRTY.
BATH WILL MAKE IT CLEAN!
Mgh...!

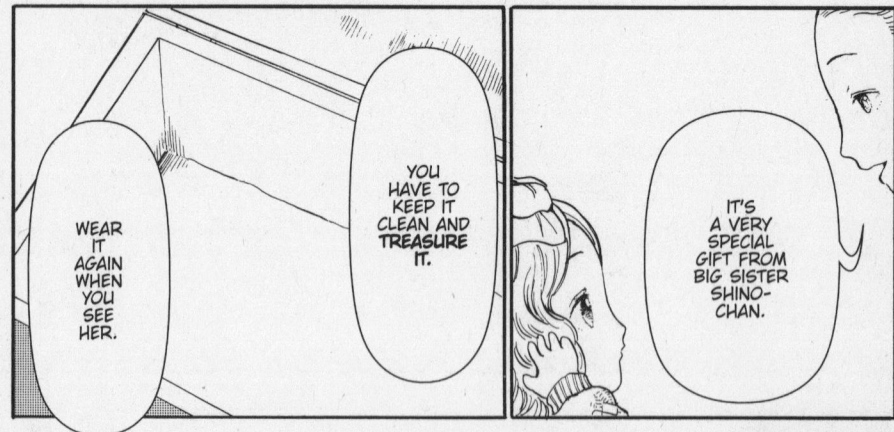

THAT'S RIGHT.	A TREASURE BOX?

KEEP IT IN HERE.

WEAR IT AGAIN WHEN YOU SEE HER.

YOU HAVE TO KEEP IT CLEAN AND **TREASURE IT**.

IT'S A VERY SPECIAL GIFT FROM BIG SISTER SHINO-CHAN.

STEAM
STEAM
YOU REALLY LIKE HER, DON'T YOU, MAKI-CHAN?
YEP!
DO YOU LOVE GOING TO PRE-SCHOOL?
UH-HUH!
NITE-NITE.
SHHK

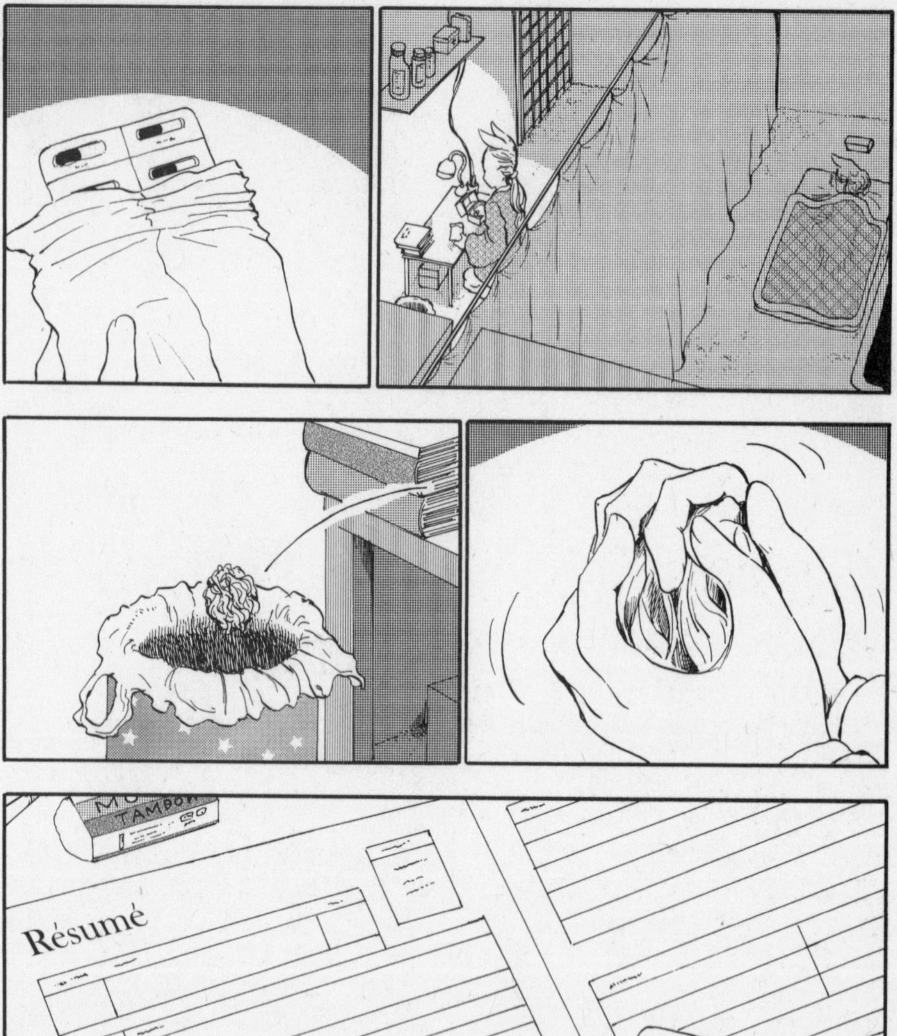
Résumé
ZEZEBRA Rabber 90

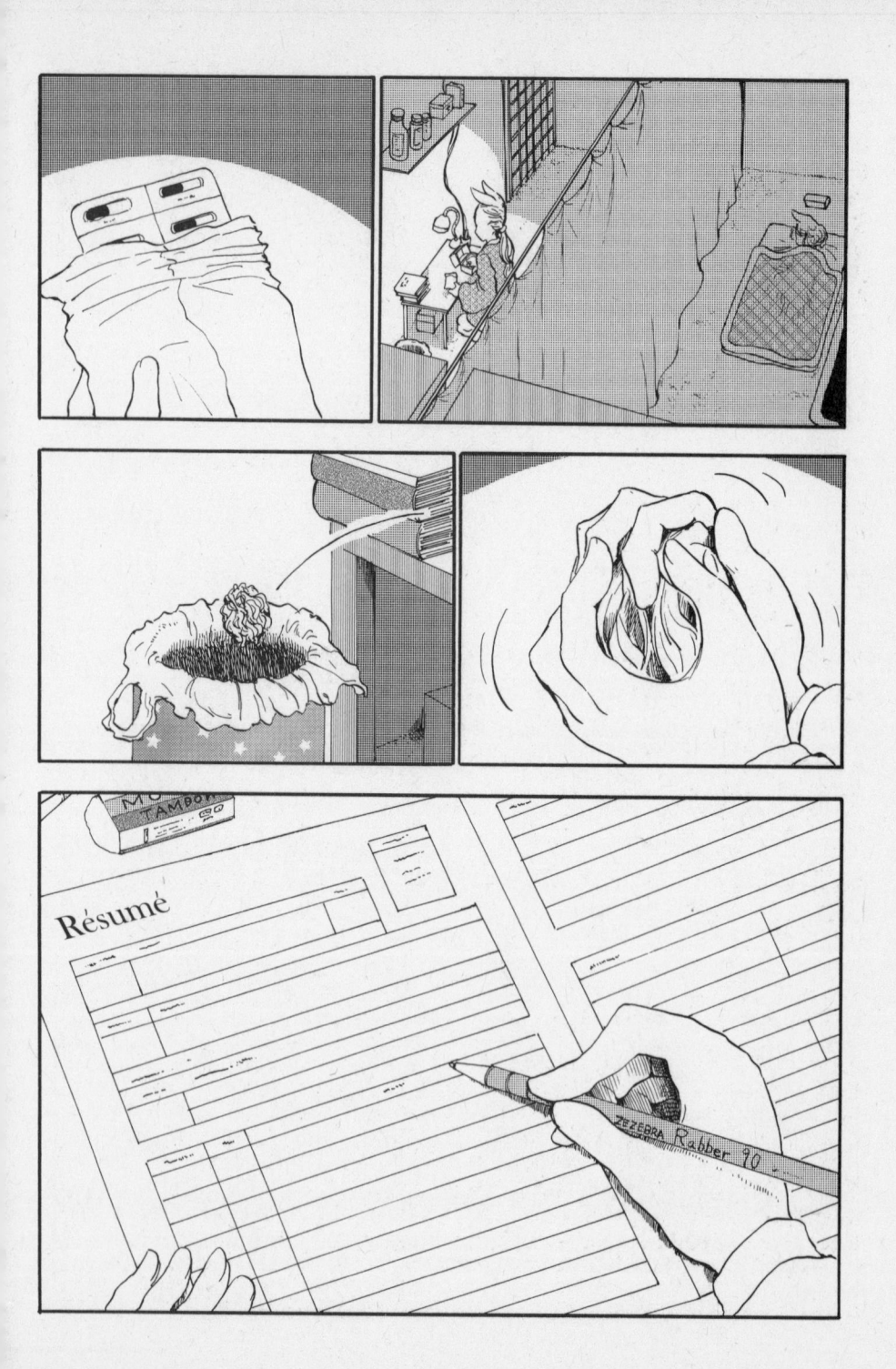

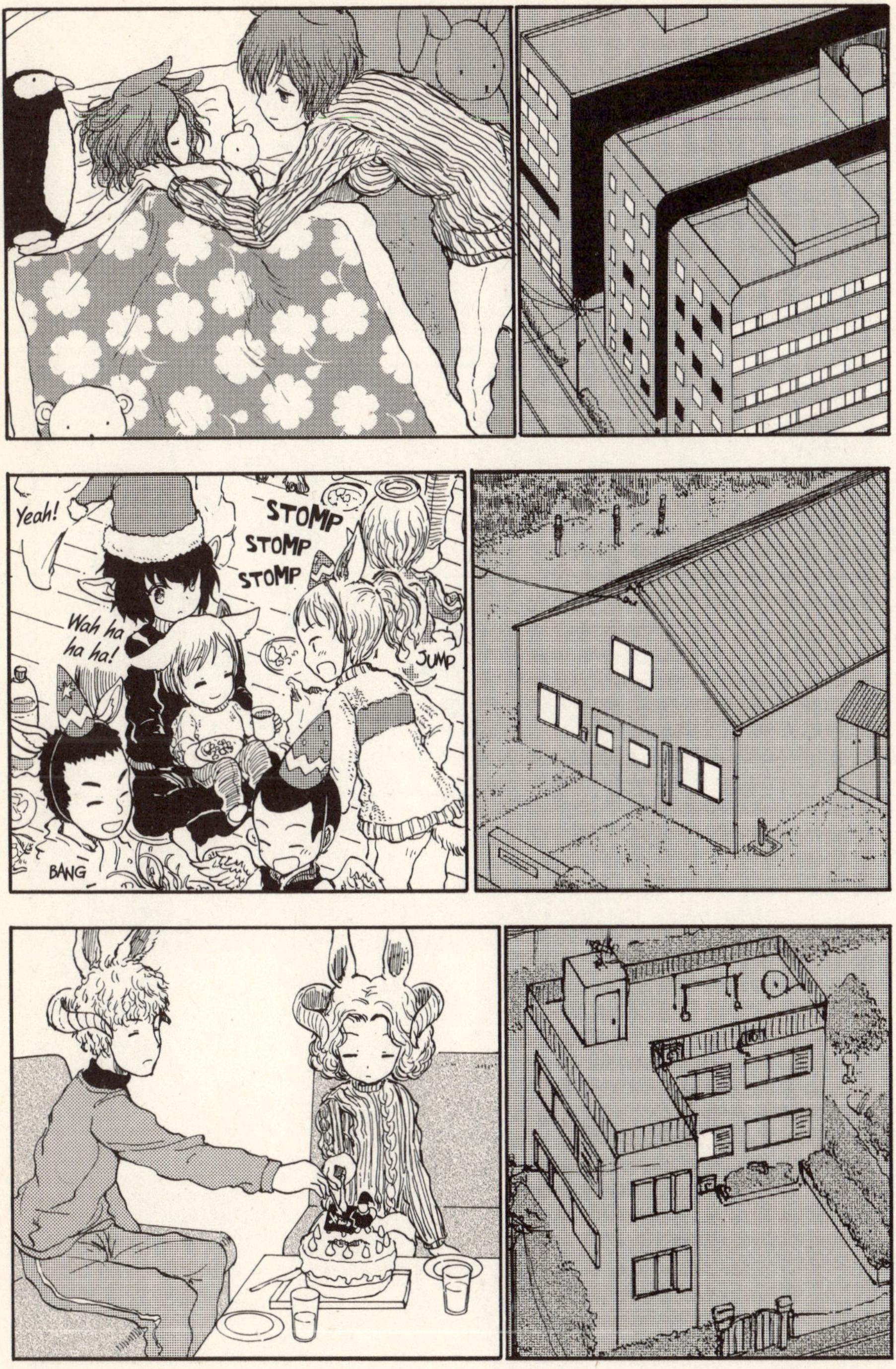
STOMP
STOMP
STOMP
Yeah!
Wah ha ha ha!
JUMP
BANG

SENSEI, AREN'T YOU DRINKING TOO MUCH?
YOU ALL SHOULD DRINK, TOO! YOU SHOULD FEEL LIKE **DRINKING** IF YOU'RE HERE!
NO, I'M UNDER-AGE.
That's a problem.
Charming
Nice!
SENSEI, THERE'S NO WAY THIS GIRL ISN'T POPULAR.
WHERE IN THE WORLD IS **HAPPINESS?**
AYAKA-CHAN, THAT'S NOT...
I'M SURE IT'S CLOSE BY!
IT'S **JUICE.** 100% FRUIT JUICE.
I'm only in middle school.

A Centaur's Life

MESOZOIC CREATURES

DINOSAURS AND THEIR CLOSE RELATIVES: THE GIGANTIFICATION OF DINOSAURS

One reason for dinosaurs' popularity, and indeed their most eye-catching trait, is surely their enormous size. The average Tyrannosaurus was estimated at thirteen meters tall, with sauropods such as the Supersaurus reaching anywhere from thirty to sixty meters tall. Of course there were also small dinosaurs such as the Compsognathus, but even they could reach up to 70 centimeters at full maturity, making them fairly large creatures, all things considered.

An advantage of their large size is that it became more difficult for other species to attack them. You may ask why, then, don't all species grow large? The answer, of course, is that different creatures have different niches to fill, meaning that there are also merits to being small. For example, hawks and lions do not compete for food with sparrows and mice, meaning that these species are not in competition over the same ecological niche. Meanwhile, young are reared and nourished by full-grown adults, meaning that they don't have to compete with smaller species.

That said, it is thought that, among dinosaurs, the young carried out the same lifestyle as the fully grown. This meant that for dinosaurs, bigger truly was better. Smaller species would wind up competing with the young of larger species over the same ecological niche, robbing smallness of any merit. Many believe that this is what led to dinosaurs growing in size as an overall group.

DIPLODOCUS

An herbivorous sauropod which thrived during the late Jurassic period. They ranged from twenty to thirty-five meters in length, with a long neck and tail. They probably used their pencil-like teeth to pull leaves from trees and swallow them whole, then used gastroliths (stomach stones) to break them down and aid digestion.

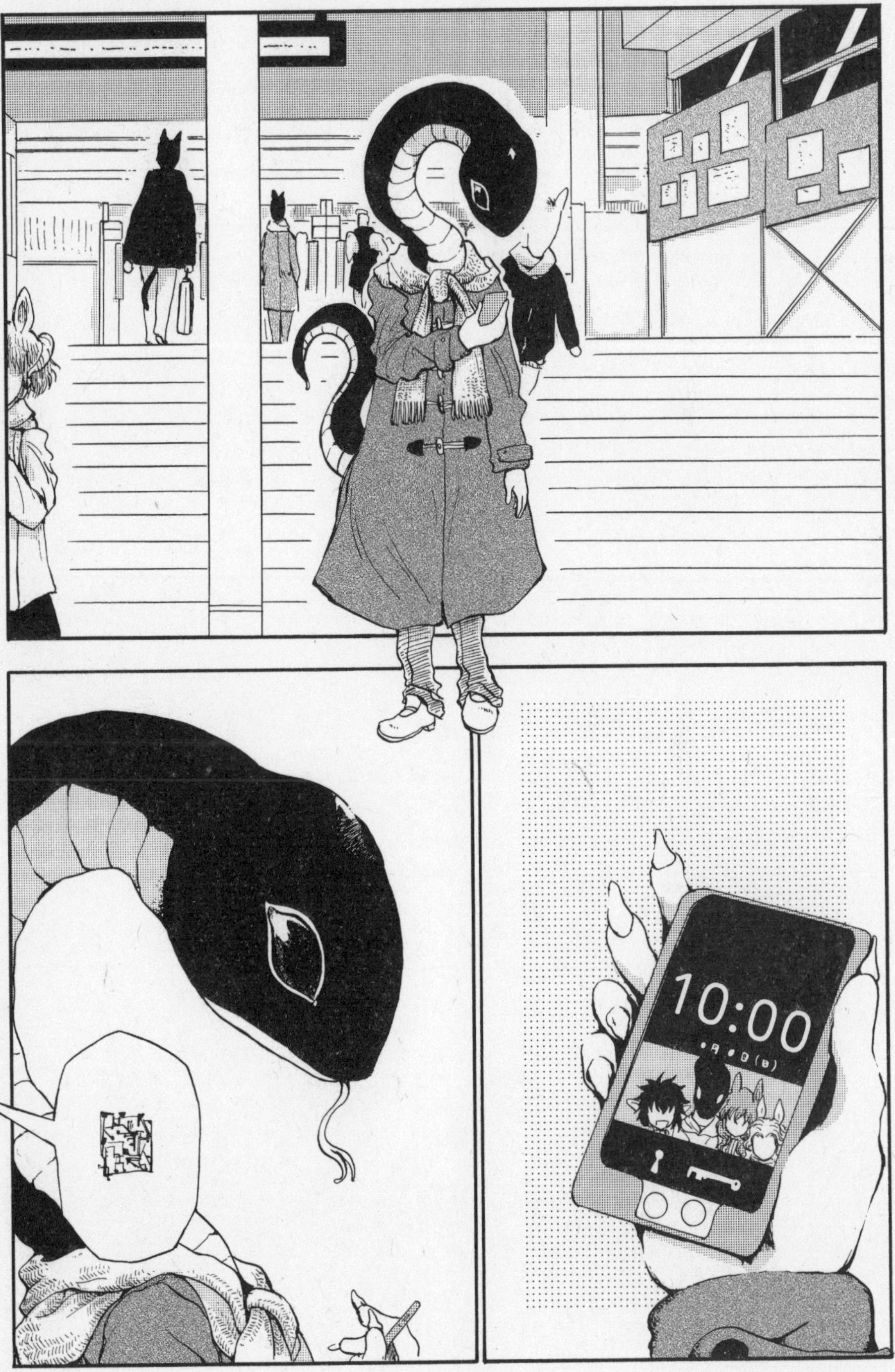
10:00

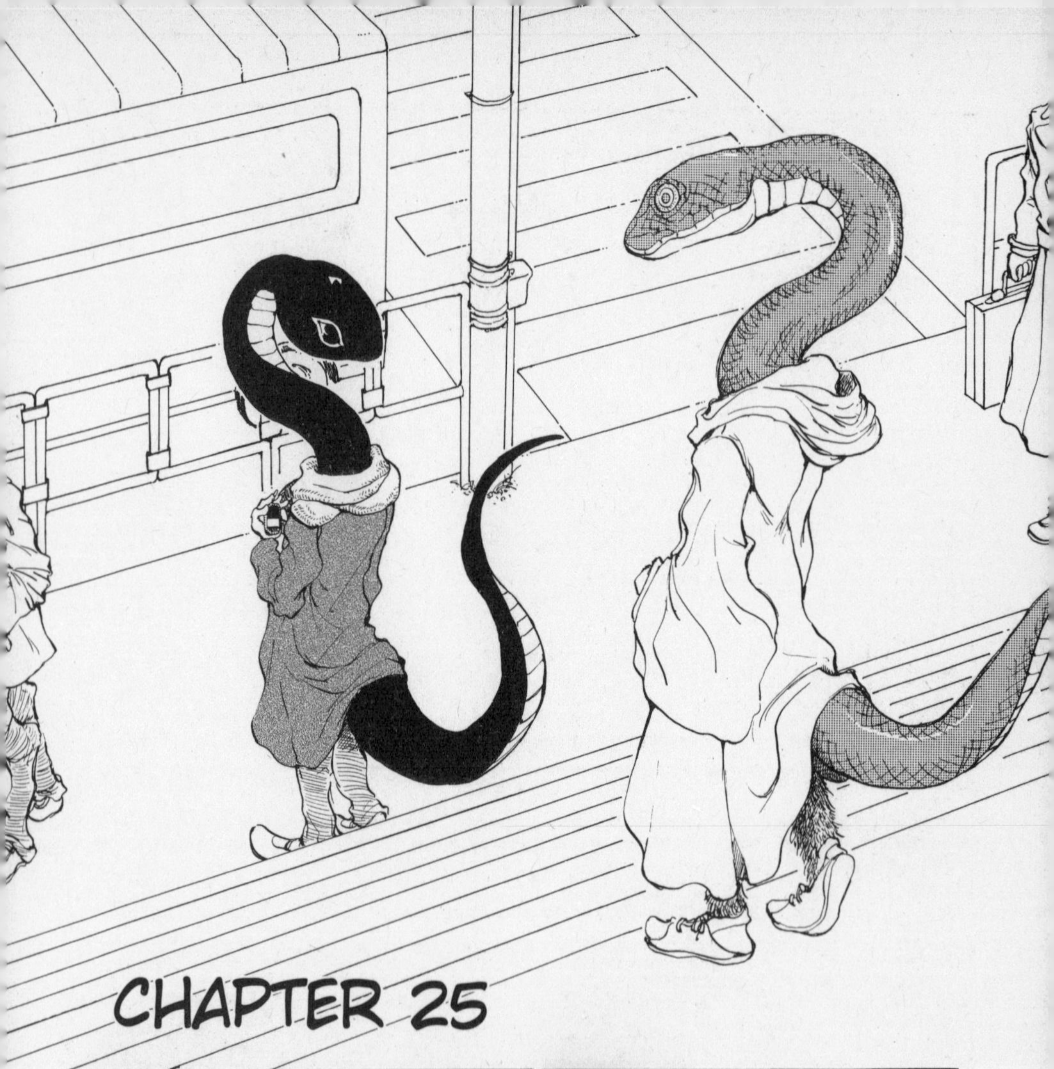

CHAPTER 25

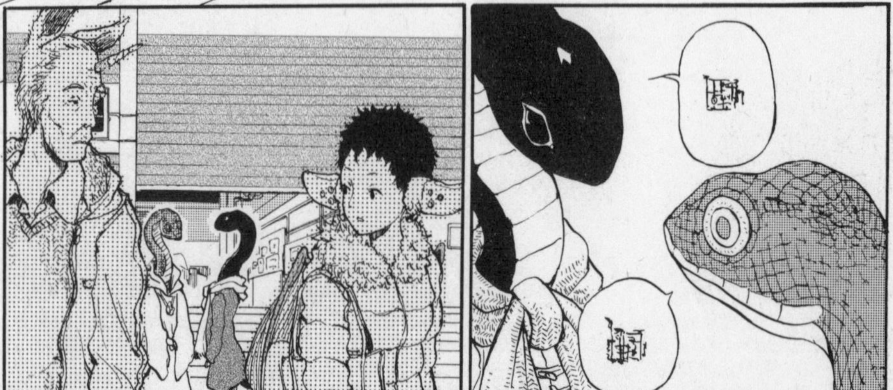

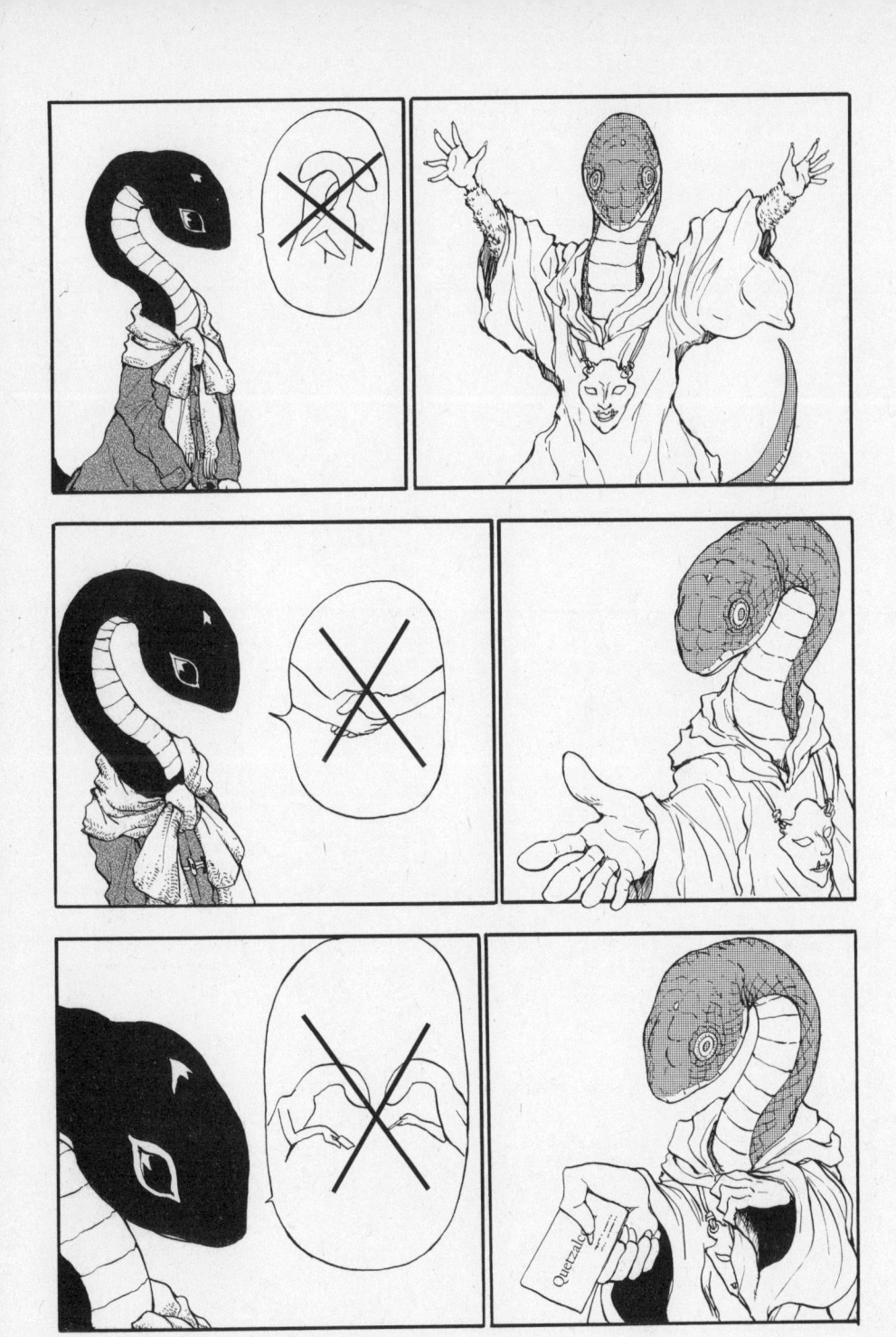

In Japan, business cards should be given with both hands.

COFFEE
WHUNK
I WOULD LIKE TO ORDER TWO COFFEES.
AH! R-RIGHT AWAY.

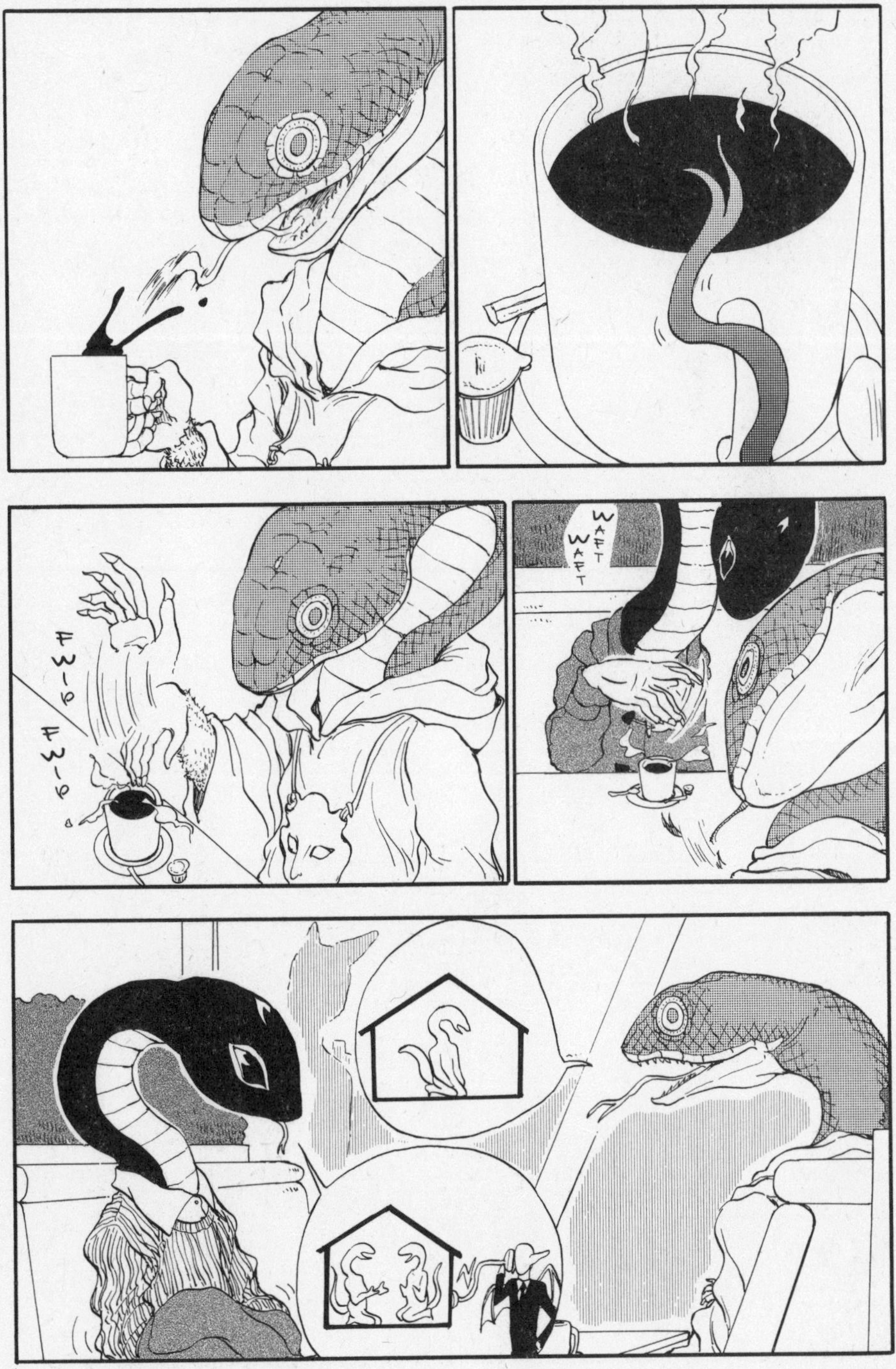
FWIP
FWIP
WAFT
WAFT

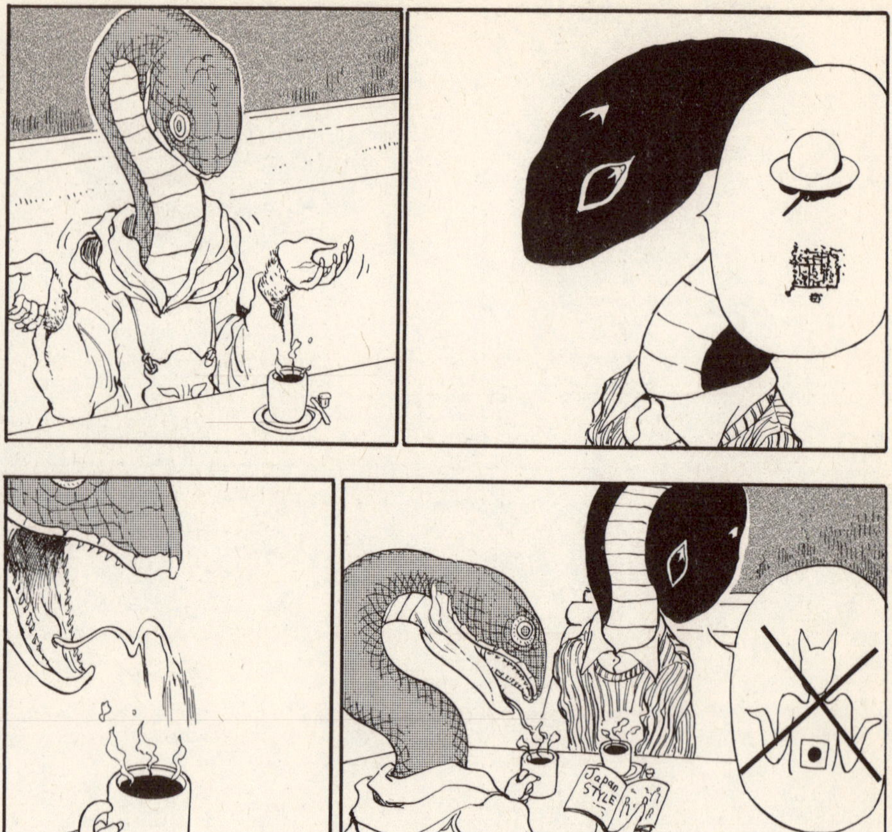
Japan STYLE
FLOP
R-18
LOVE of Antarctica

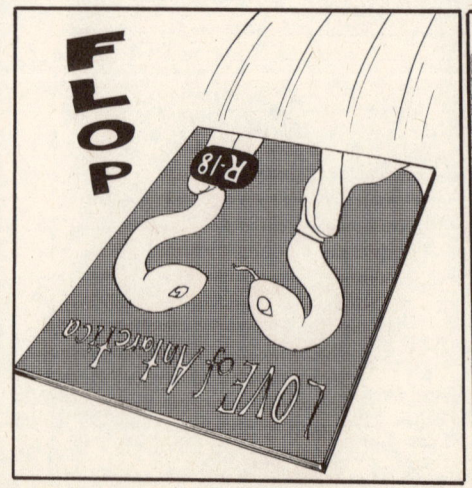

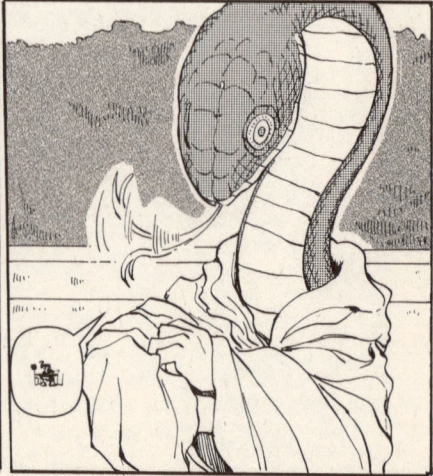

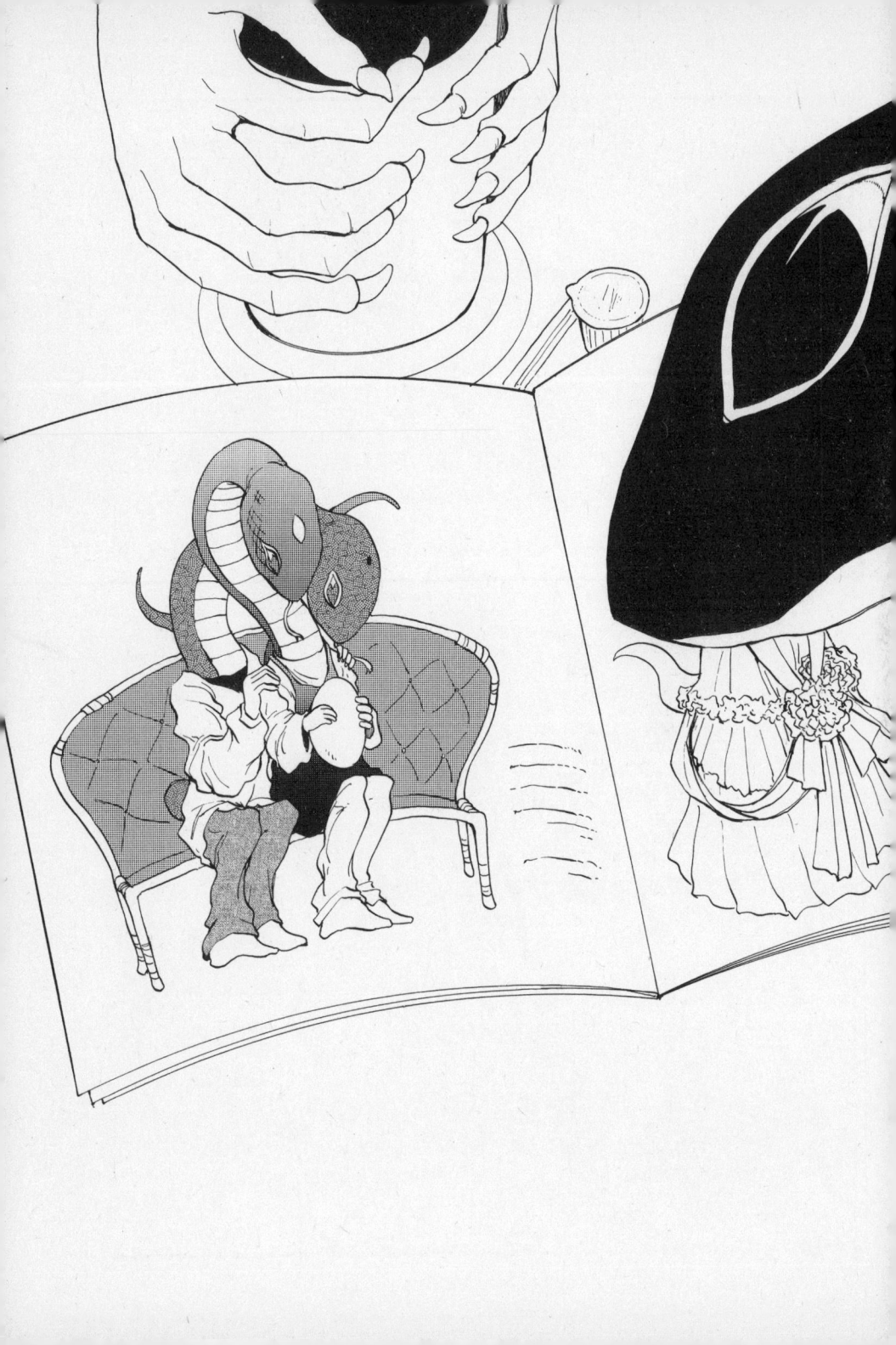

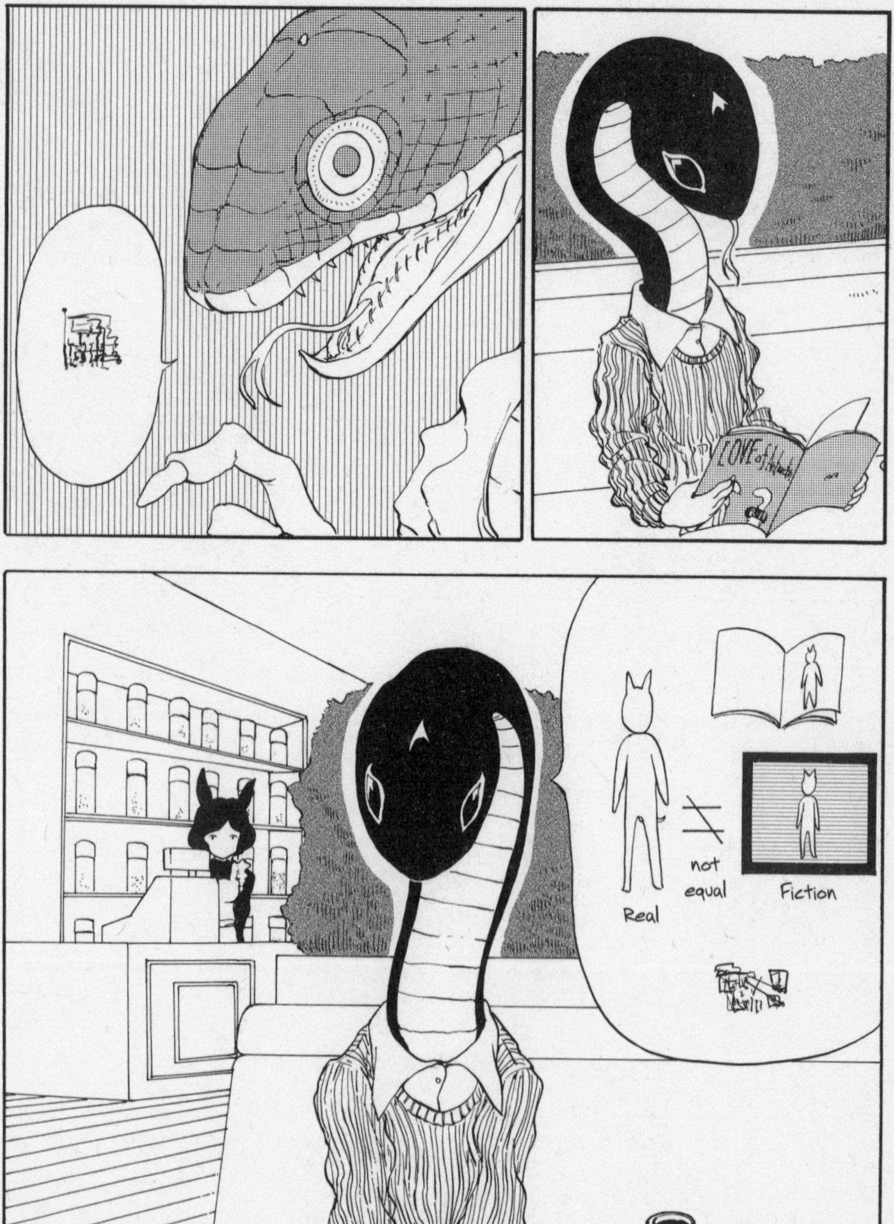
Real
not equal
Fiction

EH, THEY'RE NOT SPEAKING ENGLISH.

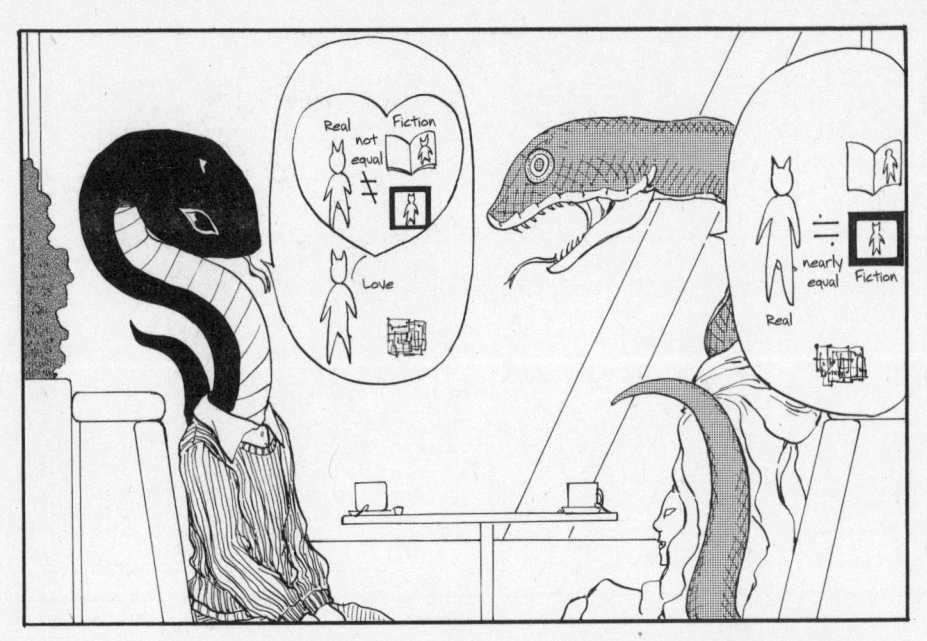

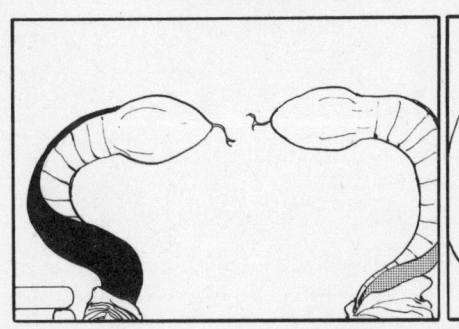

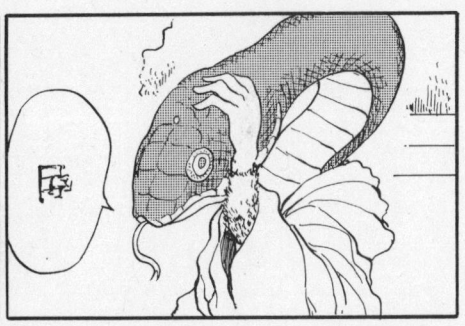

YOU SPEAK ENGLISH, DON'T YOU?

SNAP

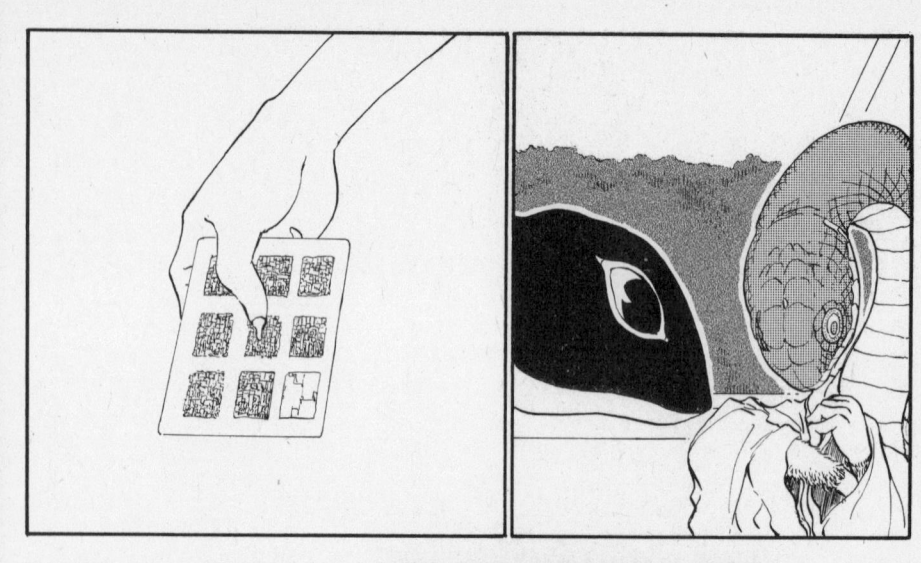

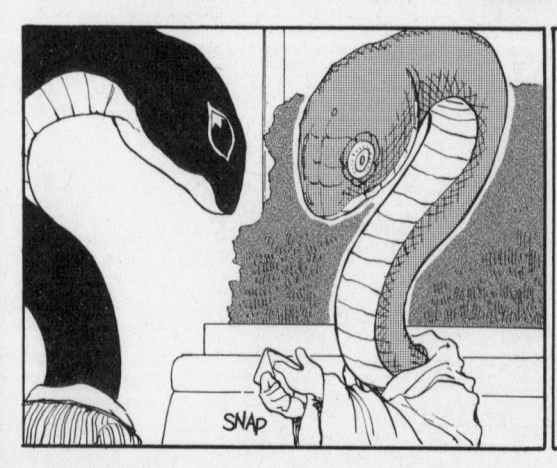

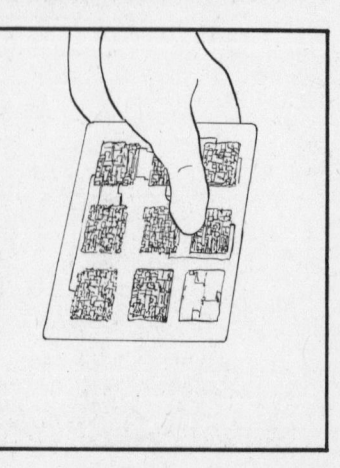

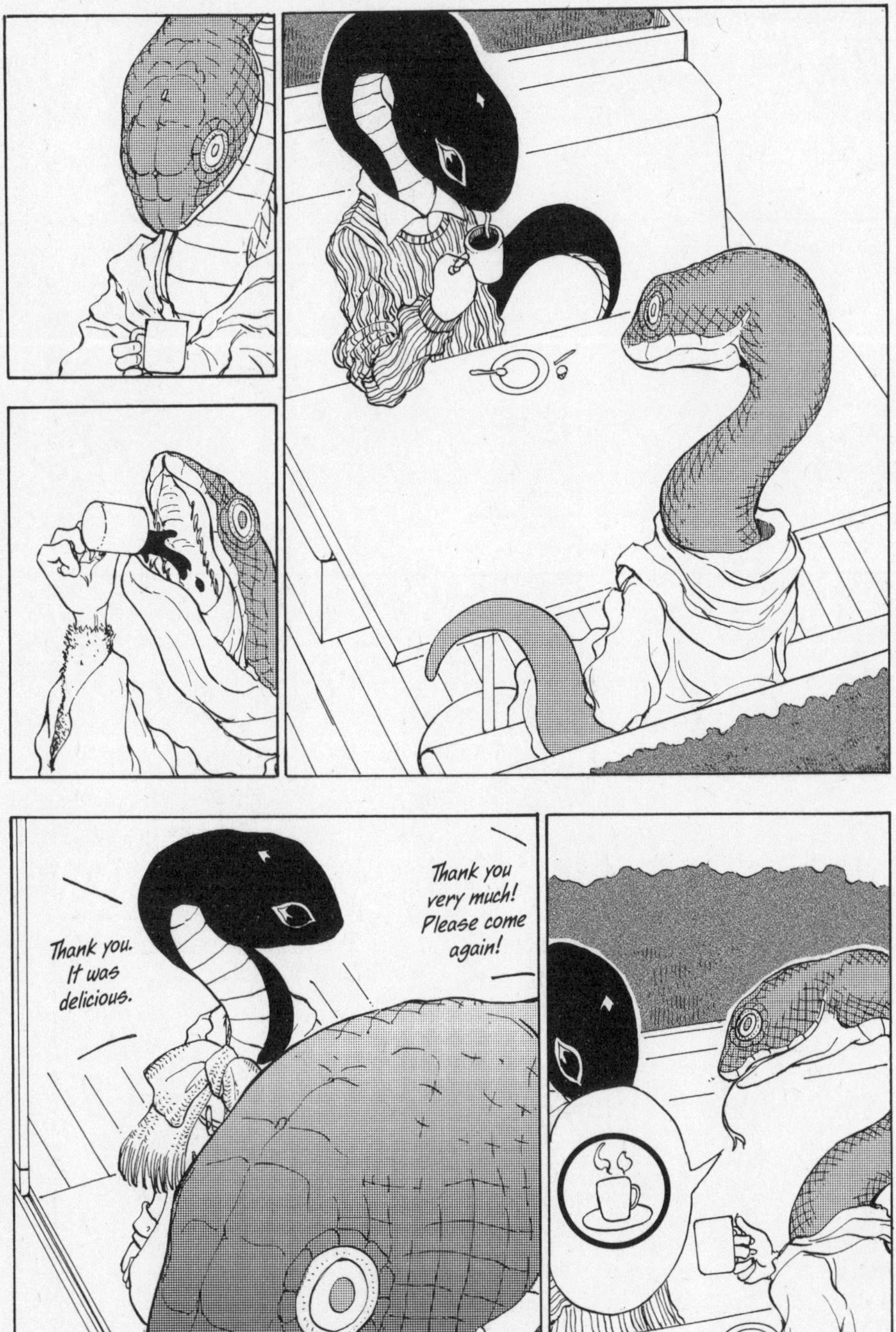
Thank you very much! Please come again!
Thank you. It was delicious.

HOW WAS IT? DID IT FEEL NOSTALGIC?	HE DID. I SEE. SO YOUR BUDDY CAME TO VISIT.
WHAT? YOU JUST SAW ME THE DAY BEFORE YESTERDAY!	HONESTLY SPEAKING, I FEEL MORE NOSTALGIC BEING WITH YOU AGAIN.

A Centaur's Life

MESOZOIC CREATURES

DINOSAURS AND THEIR CLOSE RELATIVES: DINOSAUR LINEAGE

We use the word "dinosaur" quite broadly to represent a vast variety of species, spanning several separate lineages. There are various theories on how those lineages are divided, but here we will briefly summarize the mostly commonly accepted theory.

First, dinosaurs are widely divided amongst two orders: Saurischia and Ornithischia. In general, this classification is determined by the direction of the pubic bone on the pelvis--if it points forward, they are saurischians; if it points backward, they are ornithischians.

Saurischians are furthermore divided into theropods such as the tyrannosaurus, allosaurus, and velociraptor, and sauropods like the brachiosaurus, diplodocus, and supersaurus.

Ornithischians, meanwhile, are divided into several groups: thyreophora like the stegosaurus and ankylosaurus, ornithopods such as the hadrosaur and parasaurolophus (so-called "duck-billed dinosaurs"), pachycephalosaurids such as the pachycephalosaurus (so-called "head-butting dinosaurs"), and marginocephalia, which included ceratopsians like the triceratops and styracosaurus.

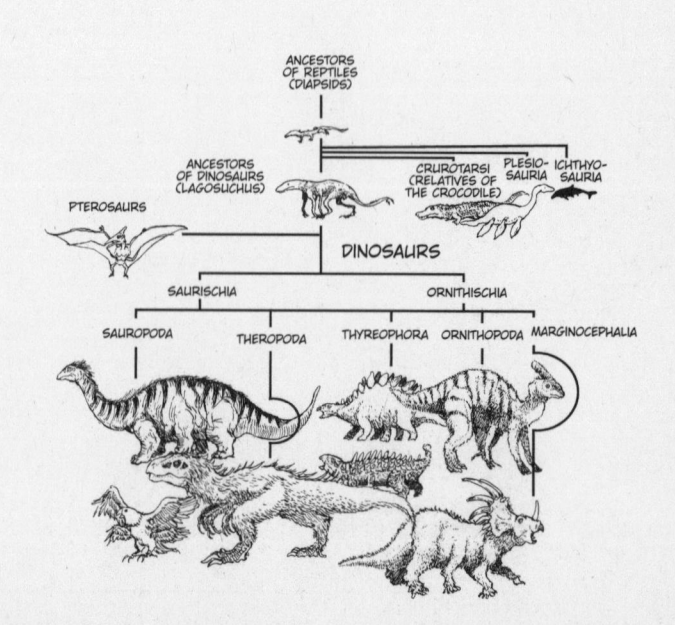

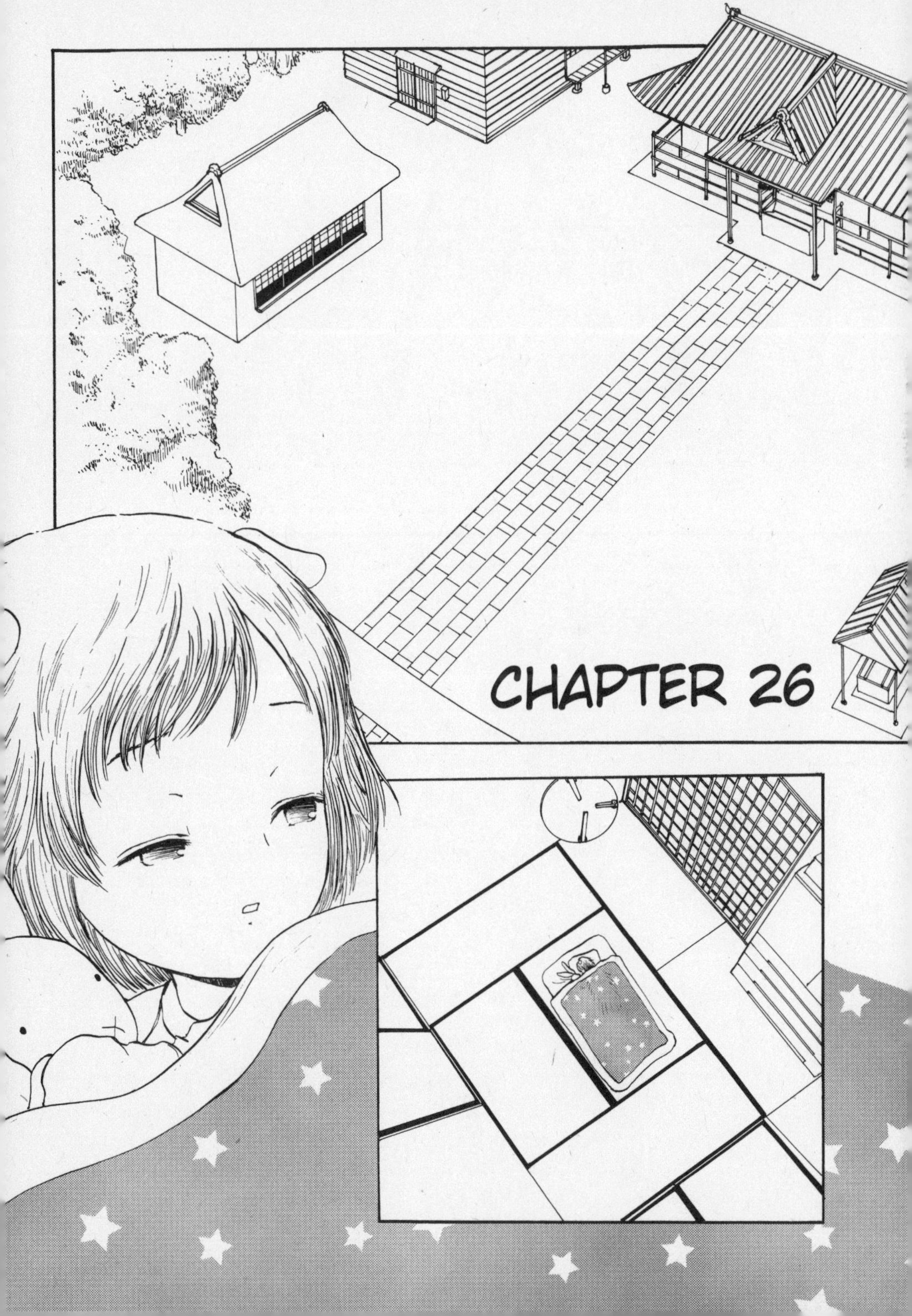
CHAPTER 26

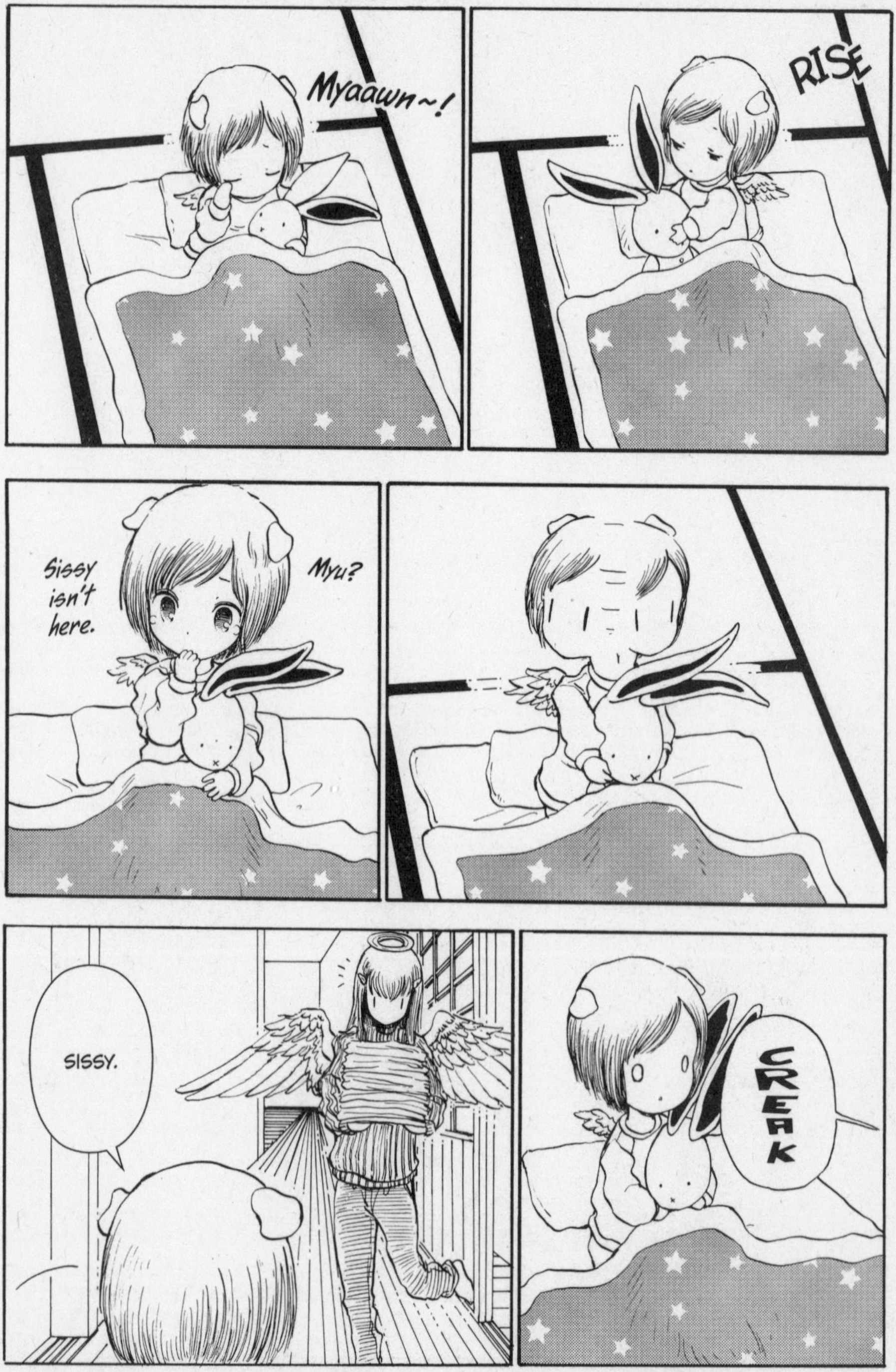
Myaawn~!
RISE
Myu?
Sissy isn't here.
SISSY.
CREAK

OH, YOU'RE AWAKE!
SQUEEZE
NOT GONNA PLAY WITH SISSY?
TODDLE TODDLE
Sue-chan's current ride

SQUEEZE
UNTIL NOW...
SHE WAS ALWAYS WITH ME.
DON'T GO OUT INTO THE STREET.
YESH.
Umph!
PEDAL
PEDAL
PEDAL

PEDAL
PEDAL
WHY THE SUDDEN INTEREST IN THE TRIKE?
Huff
Huff
OH WELL, MAYBE IT'LL BUILD UP HER STAMINA.
WE'RE HOME~!
WELCOME BACK!
PEDAL
PEDAL
SHE CAME TO GREET US WITH HER TRICYCLE!
HA HA! SUE-CHAN REALLY LOVES THAT TRI-CYCLE!

BIG SIS WILL RIDE ON A TRICYCLE, TOO!
MY LEGS HIT THE BAR...
Was it this small?
Aw, the red part is all rusty.
Myu...
SQUEAK
SQUEAK

LET'S RACE!
Myu?
THE FINISH LINE IS *WAY* OUT...
HERE!
LET'S DO IT!
Mii...
READY...
GO!

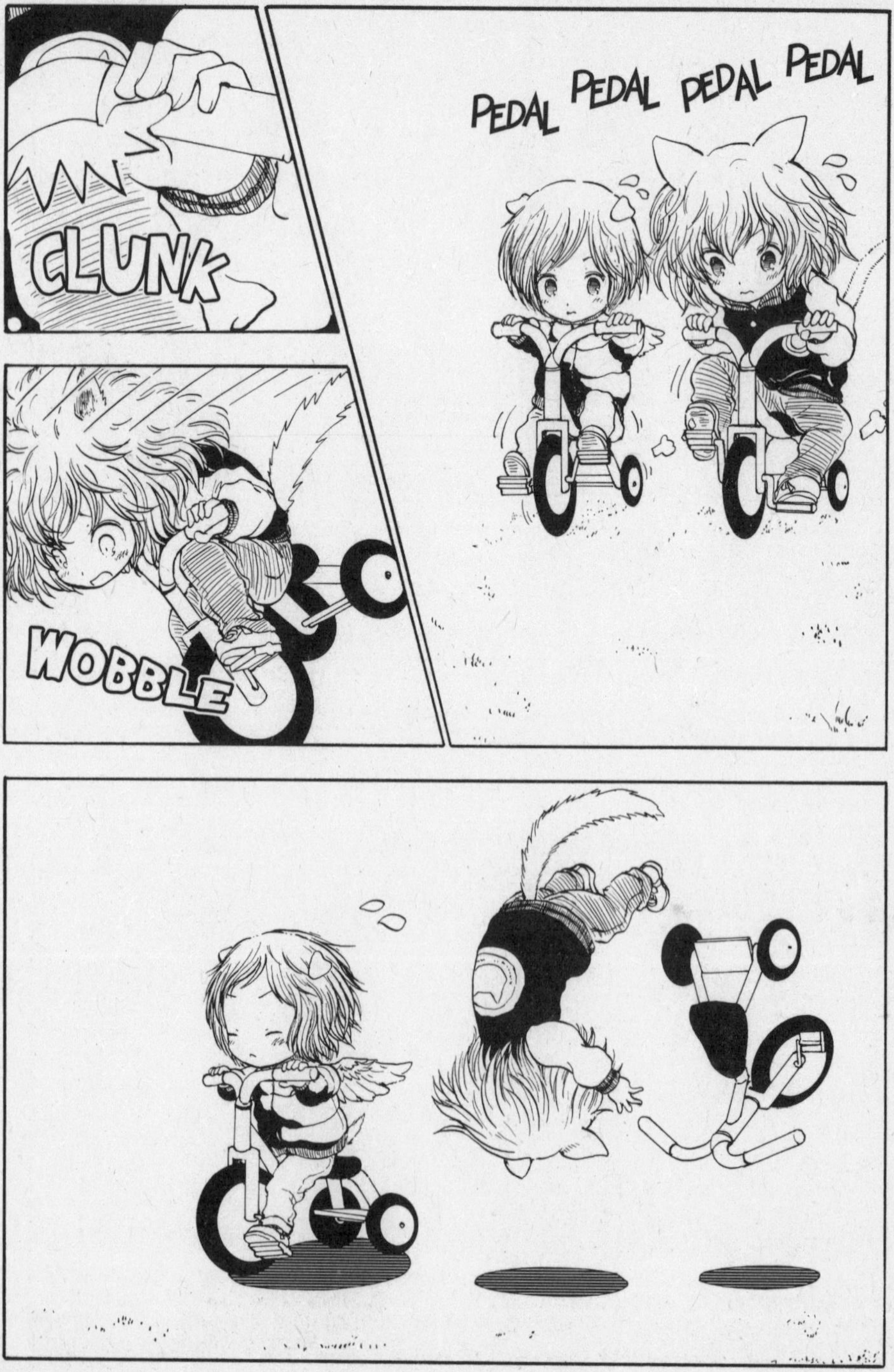
PEDAL PEDAL PEDAL PEDAL
CLUNK
WOBBLE

SUE-CHAN WINS~!
Gyah!
PEDAL PEDAL PEDAL
You okay?
Mm' yeah.
Huff
Huff
Huff

You won against big sister. Amazing!
Good job!
Now, now.
That wasn't a win...
CHI-CHANS' TRICYCLE IS ALREADY TOO SMALL.
WE NEED A **BICYCLE** RIGHT AWAY!
GRANDPA AND GRANDMA IN OSAKA WILL BUY YOU A BICYCLE WHEN SPRING ROLLS AROUND, RIGHT?
LET'S RACE WITH BICYCLES NEXT.
ABSO-LUTELY NOT!

EVERY TIME YOU GUYS DO SOMETHING DANGEROUS, MY LIFESPAN SHORTENS BY FIVE YEARS.
Boo!
Boo!
WHAT HAPPENS IF IT GETS SHORT?
BIG SISTER WILL DIE.
DIE...?
YUP, BECAUSE CHI BIG SISTERS ALWAYS DO BAD THINGS.
THAT'S NOT FAIR~!
Mii!
What do you mean?
I'M TELLING YOU, YOU GUYS HAVE A RECORD AGAINST YOU!
Chi-chans' Record
1 The first day they could walk...
2 Gone within one hour.
3 Found five hours later 20km away.
How?!
RIBBIT

PEDAL
PEDAL
PEDAL

THAT LOOKS LIKE FUN.

THAT MAKES ME SAD.

DID YOU ALREADY FORGET ME?

WHO?

Someone I know? ??

HEY, LET ME TRY THAT, TOO.

Just a little.

Not yet?
PEDAL
PEDAL
DASH
PEDAL
PEDAL
OH, YOU HAVE ANOTHER ONE?
PEDAL
PEDAL

LET'S RACE TO THAT GATE!

ALL RIGHT.

On your mark!

Get set!

GO!

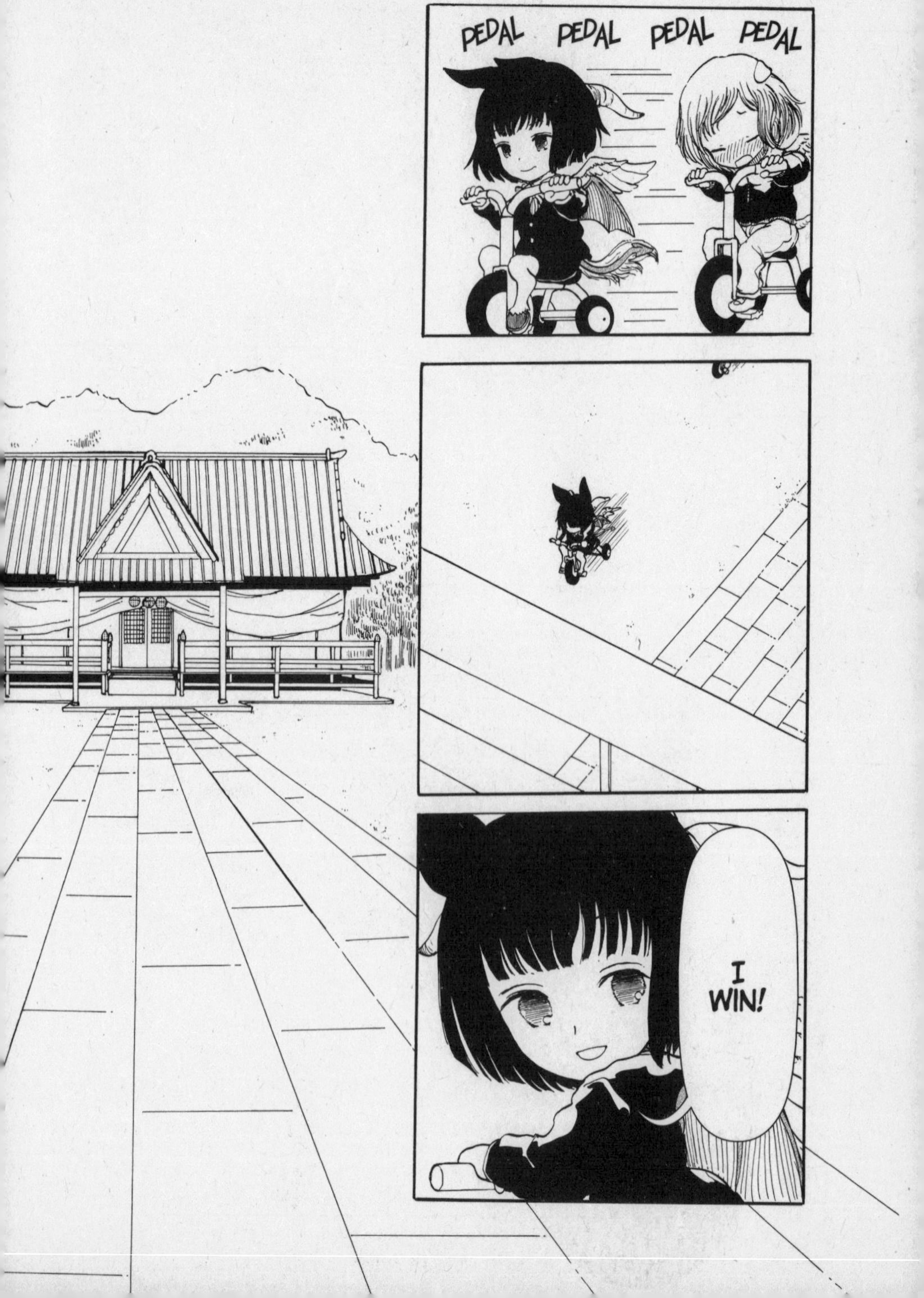
PEDAL PEDAL PEDAL PEDAL
I WIN!

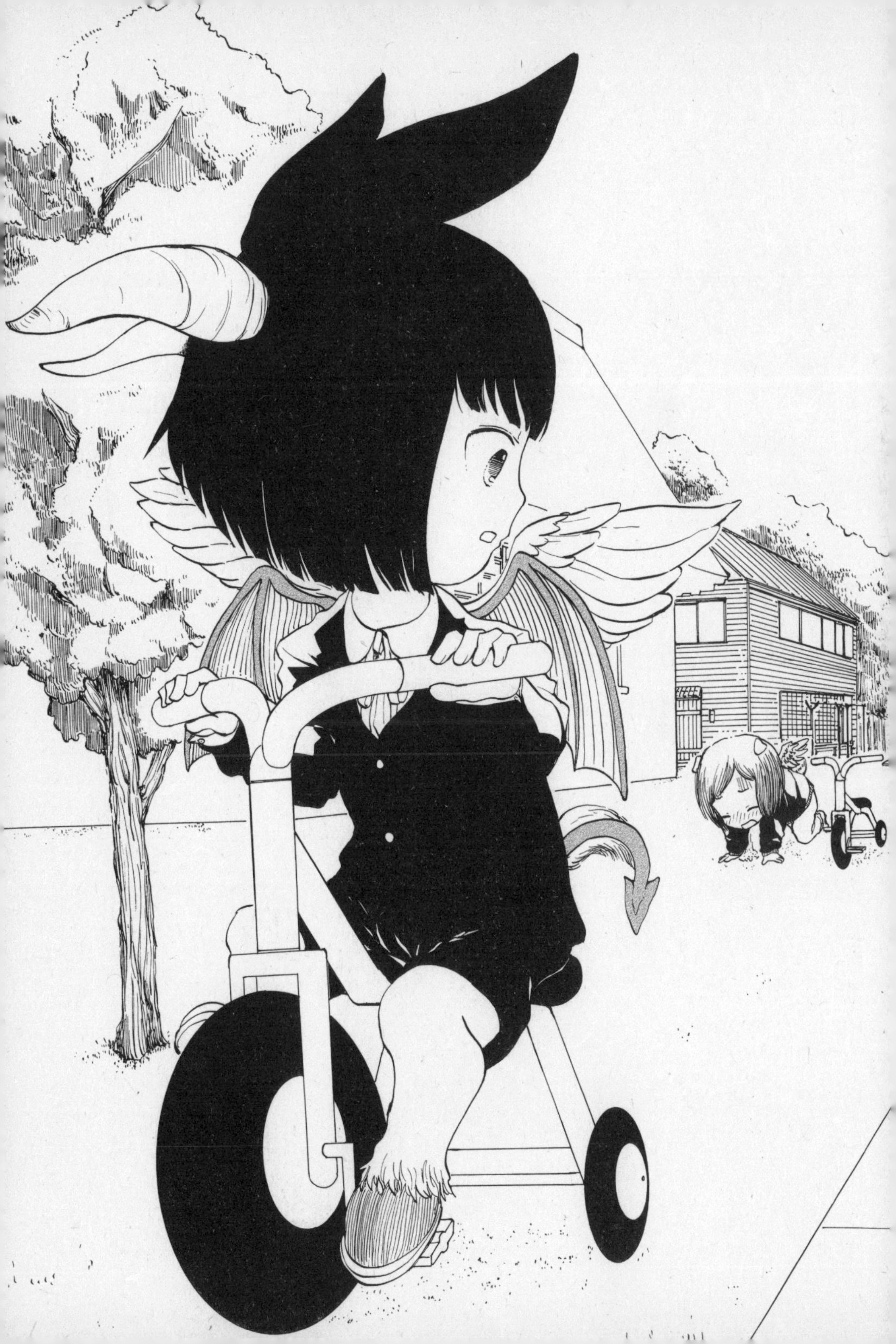

HEY, ARE YOU OKAY?

HUFF HUFF

I'M JUST GONNA GO IN.

THIS PLACE IS MINE TO BEGIN WITH.

HEY, IS ANYONE HERE?

WELL, NORMAL PEOPLE CAN'T HEAR MY VOICE ANYWAY.

DID SOMEONE COME IN?

Hm?

TAP TAP

OH, ASLEEP AGAIN?

HOW STRANGE...

SHE DOESN'T SEEM TO GET BETTER.
HMM?
WHAT'S THIS?
Peaches
WHERE DID THIS COME FROM?
??
The younger generation doesn't know that canned peaches were gifts for the sick in the past.

A Centaur's Life

MESOZOIC CREATURES

DINOSAURS AND THEIR CLOSE RELATIVES: BACKDROP TO THE WORLD OF DINOSAURS

SO DISTRACTED ARE WE BY DINOSAURS THEMSELVES THAT WE RARELY TAKE THE TIME TO CONSIDER WHAT COMPRISED THEIR BACKDROP-- THAT IS, THE PLANT LIFE OF THE MESOZOIC ERA. IT SEEMS THAT LOW-BUDGET FILMS TEND TO SIMPLY USE MODERN-DAY PLANTS, WHILE POPULAR LITERATURE OFTEN CONTAINS ILLUSTRATIONS OF FERNS.

IF THERE'S ONE TYPE OF FLORA REPRESENTATIVE OF THE MESOZOIC, HOWEVER, IT'S GYMNOSPERM. GYMNOSPERM PLANTS--RELATIVES OF MODERN CONIFERS (NEEDLE-LEAFED TREES) SUCH AS CYCAS, PINES, AND CEDARS, AS WELL AS GINGKO TREES--HAD ALREADY MADE THEIR ENTRANCE BY THE MESOZOIC'S CARBONIFEROUS PERIOD. FERNS, WHICH PROPAGATE THROUGH THE RELEASE OF THIRSTY SPORES, STRUGGLED TO PROLIFERATE. GYMNOSPERM SEEDS, HOWEVER, REQUIRE FAR LESS MOISTURE, AND THUS WERE ABLE TO GAIN A FIRM FOOTHOLD. BY THE TRIASSIC AND INTO THE JURASSIC, FERNS HAD BEEN CORDONED OFF TO THE DAMP RECESSES OF SWAMPLANDS, WHILE GYMNOSPERM FORESTS GREW FAR AND WIDE.

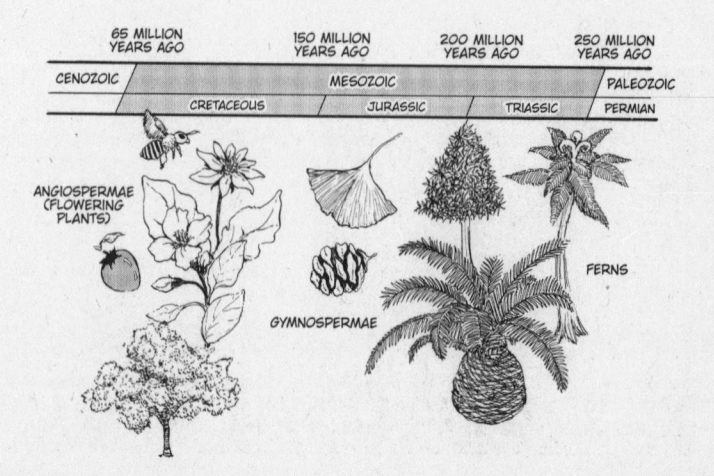

	65 MILLION YEARS AGO	150 MILLION YEARS AGO	200 MILLION YEARS AGO	250 MILLION YEARS AGO
CENOZOIC		MESOZOIC		PALEOZOIC
	CRETACEOUS	JURASSIC	TRIASSIC	PERMIAN

ANGIOSPERMAE (FLOWERING PLANTS)

GYMNOSPERMAE

FERNS

CHAPTER 27

KIMIHARA-SAN AND GOKURAKU-SAN...

NEITHER OF YOU HAVE TURNED IN YOUR CAREER SURVEY.

EXCUSE ME. MAY I HAVE A MOMENT?

YOU ALREADY TURNED YOURS IN, KYOKO?
A LONG TIME AGO. I ALREADY KNOW WHAT I WANT TO DO.
OH? WHAT'S THAT?
I'M GOING TO STUDY LAW AT FIRST IMPERIAL.
THAT'S AMAZING! ARE YOU CONFIDENT YOU'LL GET IN?
NOT CONFIDENT, BUT I THINK IT'S POSSIBLE IF I WORK HARD.
I DON'T WANT TO STAY HERE FOREVER. I WANT TO TEST MY SKILL AGAINST THE WORLD.
STUDYING ISN'T THE *ONLY* SKILL THERE IS, YA KNOW.
BUT GRADUATING FROM A GOOD SCHOOL DEFINITELY OPENS MORE DOORS FOR US.

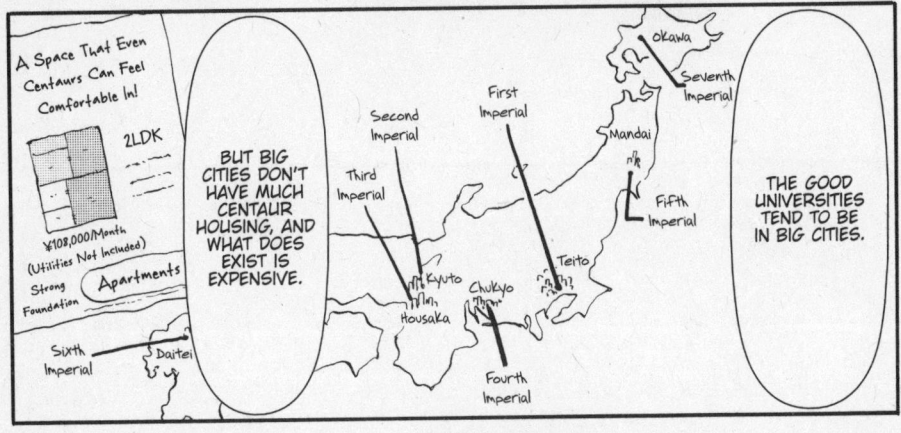

GETTING IN IS ONLY PART OF THE PROBLEM FOR ME.

HIME, YOUR GPA IS HIGHER THAN MINE. WHAT ABOUT YOU?

BUT BIG CITIES DON'T HAVE MUCH CENTAUR HOUSING, AND WHAT DOES EXIST IS EXPENSIVE.

THE GOOD UNIVERSITIES TEND TO BE IN BIG CITIES.

A Space That Even Centaurs Can Feel Comfortable In!
2LDK
¥108,000/Month
(Utilities Not Included)
Strong Foundation
Apartments

Okawa
Seventh Imperial
First Imperial
Second Imperial
Mandai
Third Imperial
Fifth Imperial
Kyuto
Housaka
Chukyo
Teito
Sixth Imperial
Daitei
Fourth Imperial

Ggah?!

THAT LAW DOESN'T APPLY TO OLD BUILDINGS, THOUGH.

PUBLIC FACILITIES ARE DIFFERENT, BUT...

THE EQUALITY LAWS SAY ALL BUILDINGS HAVE TO BE ACCESSIBLE.

AND THERE ARE TIMES WE ARE REFUSED BECAUSE OF OUR SIZE.

THERE ARE PLACES WE PHYSICALLY CAN'T FIT.

MY FATHER SAYS I SHOULD JUST GO TO **KANA UNIVERSITY** HERE.
WELL, IT'S NOT LIKE YOU **HAVE** TO GO TO COLLEGE.
KANA UNIVERSITY IS AN IMPERIAL UNIVERSITY, SO IT'S NOT A BAD CHOICE.
IT'S HARD TO GET A JOB AFTER GRADUATING FROM A NEWLY ESTABLISHED SCHOOL, THOUGH.
BUT ACTUALLY, THE MAIN PROBLEM IS I HAVE NO CONFIDENCE OR MOTIVATION TO MOVE UPWARDS.
IF YOU'RE WORRIED ABOUT A JOB, WASN'T THAT OLD MAN FROM INTERNAL AFFAIRS TRYING TO RECRUIT YOU?
NO WAY! THAT WAS A CALL FOR **SOLDIERS** TO JOIN A FRONTLINE ARMY.

Internal Affairs Special Task Force

EXEMPLARY CITIZEN ENCOURAGEMENT STICK

FOR PEACE

HIME, DON'T GET SUCKERED IN. THOSE KINDS OF JOBS ARE ONLY COOL IN BOOKS AND MOVIES.

DON'T WORRY.

Nnngh!

THERE'S NO WAY I'D BE ABLE TO DO A JOB LIKE THAT.

LIKE I SAID, IT'S NOT FOR ME.

Well, being a regular civil servant would be kind of nice.

IF YOU REALLY WANT TO DO THAT, TAKE THE HIGHER CIVIL SERVICE EXAM.

THERE'S A LOT TO THINK ABOUT.

"Nozomi-sensei, hurry!"

A LOT OF OUR STUDENTS ARE LITTLE KIDS.

THE PROBLEM IS *WHERE* I WANT TO GO.

WHAT ABOUT YOU, NOZOMI-CHAN? YOU'LL GO TO COLLEGE EVEN IF YOU TAKE OVER THE DOJO, RIGHT?

OSU!

BUT ALL THE OTHER TEACHERS LOOK SO **SCARY**.

THEY'RE NOT REALLY GOOD WITH KIDS.

SO IF I MOVE AWAY... WELL, YOU GET THE IDEA.

WHAT ABOUT THAT GUY FROM BEFORE?
SHIGETOKI-SAN? HE ALREADY HAS A JOB.
AND HE ONLY **LOOKS** LIKE A NICE GUY.
You guys are all lazy bums!
WHY DON'T YOU STUDY PHYS ED AT KANA UNIVERSITY?
PHYS ED?
THAT SOUNDS NICE. IT'S A GOOD WAY TO SHARPEN YOUR SKILLS AND BUILD YOU UP AS A TEACHER.
WELL, IT'S NOT LIKE I **WANT** TO TAKE OVER THE DOJO.
And I don't really want to stay in my hometown forever.
YOU DON'T HAVE TO THINK ABOUT THAT RIGHT NOW.

WHAT ARE YOU GOING TO DO, CLASS PRESIDENT?

FIRST IMPERIAL, AS EXPECTED?

BUT WE MIGHT BE ABLE TO GO TO THE SAME UNIVERSITY.

AND I DON'T REALLY WANT TO DO SOMETHING JUST BECAUSE SOMEONE ELSE RECOMMENDED IT.

......

BECAUSE OF MY LITTLE SISTERS.

WHEN I GRADUATE, MY LITTLE SISTERS WON'T EVEN BE TEN YEARS OLD.

I DO.

EVEN THE CLASS PRESIDENT WORRIES ABOUT THIS.

GET OFF OF THAT!

THEY'RE NOT OLD ENOUGH TO TAKE CARE OF THEM- SELVES.

MY FATHER CAN'T TAKE CARE OF THEM ON HIS OWN.

And who would look after my father?

I'VE THOUGHT ABOUT DEPENDING ON MY FATHER'S PARENTS...

MNCH

MNCH

AND THERE'S A RISK THEY'D GET TOO SPOILED.

BUT NO MATTER HOW *CUTE* THEIR GRAND- CHILDREN ARE, IT'S DIFFICULT TO TAKE CARE OF THEM.

"EVERYTHING WOULD FALL TO PIECES."

"IF THAT HAPPENED, I WOULD BREAK DOWN."

"MY GRANDPARENTS ARE HEALTHY NOW, BUT WHO KNOWS WHEN *THEY'LL* NEED TO BE TAKEN CARE OF?"

"I DON'T LIKE TO THINK ABOUT IT..."

"IF I TAKE A LEAVE OF ABSENCE, I CAN GRADUATE WHEN THE TRIPLETS START MIDDLE SCHOOL."

"I WOULD HAVE TO TRAVEL LONG DISTANCES TO AND FROM SCHOOL. THE OTHER OPTION IS TO STUDY LAW AT KANA UNIVERSITY."

"IT'S HOPELESS."

"REGARDLESS OF WHETHER IT'S A GOOD SCHOOL..."

"IT'S DEFINITELY THE MOST PRESTIGIOUS."

"FIRST IMPERIAL SEEMS REALLY IMPORTANT TO YOU."

"THEN, I'LL GO TO GRADUATE SCHOOL AT FIRST IMPERIAL."

I WANT TO HAVE THE CONNECTIONS AND OPPORTUNITIES I NEED TO **CHANGE** SOCIETY.
BUT ARE YOU THINKING A LITTLE TOO GRAND?
OH, BE QUIET!
I DON'T WANT SIT AROUND TALKING, WAITING FOR *OTHER PEOPLE* TO CHANGE THINGS!
AMAZ-ING.
BUT... I THINK IT MIGHT BE BETTER FOR ME TO GO INTO MEDICINE.

I DON'T EVEN KNOW WHAT I DON'T KNOW.

I DON'T REALLY UNDERSTAND WHAT'S WRONG WITH HER.

BUT SHE'S NOT HEALTHY, EITHER.

NOT EXACTLY.

IS SUE-CHAN THAT SICK?

YOU REALLY CARE FOR YOUR LITTLE SISTER.

SO AT THE VERY LEAST, I WANT TO BE IN A POSITION TO UNDERSTAND THE SITUATION.

EVEN IF SHE DIED TODAY...

Though, I don't want to even think of that happening.

I DON'T KNOW WHETHER THAT WOULD BE KINDEST FOR HER IN THE END.

IT'S NOT JUST THAT.

BUT IT WOULD BE HARD FOR ME.

VERY, VERY HARD.

EVEN IF IT'S PURELY SELFISH.

THAT'S WHY I WANT TO DO ANYTHING I CAN FOR MY LITTLE SISTERS.

IN THE END, THIS IS JUST MY OWN GREEDY DESIRE.

IT'S NOBODY ELSE'S RESPONSIBILITY.

WELL, THAT CONVERSATION GOT A LITTLE HEAVY.

FOR NOW, CAN YOU TWO HAND IN YOUR CAREER SURVEYS?

THIS FORM ISN'T FINAL. JUST PUT SOMETHING DOWN.

I BROUGHT AN EXTRA FORM FOR YOU, JUST IN CASE.

UGH, WHERE DID I PUT THAT THING?

THANKS.

HERE.

SHE'S AMAZING.
SHE'S SO MUCH MORE MATURE THAN US.
I'M ACTUALLY A LITTLE **JEALOUS.**
SHE HAS A REAL GOAL IN MIND.
IT'S NOT AS EASY AS IT LOOKS.
OTHERS WOULD HAVE BEEN **CRUSHED** BY THE PRESSURE.
I KNOW THAT, BUT...

I WOULDN'T HAVE TO WORRY IF THERE WAS ONLY STRAWBERRY SHORTCAKE, OR ONLY CHEESECAKE.

HOW SHOULD I PUT THIS?

THAT'S TRUE, BUT...

HIME, YOU WOULDN'T KNOW WHAT TO DO WITH FREE TIME.

EVEN IF I COULD, I'D PROBABLY BE AT A LOSS LIKE HIMENO-SAN.

MY PEOPLE DON'T HAVE THE FREEDOM TO CHOOSE OUR OWN FUTURES TO BEGIN WITH.

SUU-CHAN HAS BEEN PRETTY QUIET TODAY.

FREEDOM IS A HEAVY BURDEN, BUT YOU DON'T HAVE TO MAKE YOUR CHOICES YET. THINK IT OVER CAREFULLY.

AND AFTERWARDS, YOU'D WONDER IF THE OTHER MIGHT HAVE BEEN BETTER.

BUT IF BOTH WERE OPTIONS, YOU'D HAVE TO PICK.

A Centaur's Life

MESOZOIC CREATURES

DINOSAURS AND THEIR CLOSE RELATIVES: NON-DINOSAUR REPTILES OF THE MESOZOIC

OFTEN EXHIBITED ALONGSIDE AND MISTAKEN FOR DINOSAURS ARE PTEROSAURS, PLESIOSAURS, AND ICHTHYOSAURS. OF THE THREE, PTEROSAURS ARE PARTICULARLY CLOSE RELATIVES TO DINOSAURS, WITH WHOM THEY SHARE A COMMON ANCESTOR IN THE LAGOSUCHUS CREATURES OF THE TRIASSIC PERIOD. PLESIOSAURS, MEANWHILE, ARE CLOSER RELATED TO THE LIKES OF SCALY LIZARDS AND SNAKES (LEPIDOSAUROMORPHS) THAN THEY ARE TO DINOSAURS (OR "ARCHOSAURS," WHICH ALSO INCLUDE CROCODILES AND TURTLES). ICHTHYOSAURS, THOUGH ALSO DIAPSIDS, ARE ONLY DISTANTLY RELATED TO BOTH LIZARDS AND DINOSAURS, HAVING BRANCHED OFF EARLIER THAN EITHER OF THE ABOVE.

PTEROSAURS, SUCH AS THE WELL-KNOWN PTERANODON, WERE CREATURES CAPABLE OF POWERED FLIGHT, AND THEY DOMINATED THE SKIES DURING THE MESOZOIC AGE. HOWEVER, BY THE END OF THE CRETACEOUS PERIOD, JUST AS BIRD SPECIES WERE ALSO COMING TO MASTER POWERED FLIGHT, VIRTUALLY ALL PTEROSAURS HAD GROWN LARGE IN SIZE, AND THEY WERE ALMOST COMPLETELY WIPED OUT ALONGSIDE THE DINOSAURS.

PLESIOSAURS WERE WATER-DWELLING REPTILES, INCLUDING THE PLESIOSAURUS AND FUTABASAURUS. PLESIOSAURS WERE DIVIDED INTO TWO MAIN GROUPS--PLESIOSAUROIDEA, WHICH HAD LONG NECKS AND SMALL HEADS; AND PLIOSAUROIDEA, WHICH CONVERSELY HAD SHORT NECKS AND LARGE HEADS. BOTH HAD SIX FLIPPERS AND WERE PERFECTLY ADAPTED FOR THE LIFE AQUATIC. THE PLESIOSAURS WERE INDEED WIPED OUT ALONGSIDE THE DINOSAURS.

ICHTHYOSAURS WERE AQUATIC REPTILES EVEN FURTHER ADAPTED FOR AQUATIC LIFE AND HIGHLY SIMILAR IN FORM TO DOLPHINS. THEY ALSO RESEMBLED DOLPHINS IN THAT THEY BORE LIVE YOUNG AND GAVE BIRTH UNDERWATER. HOWEVER, UNLIKE DOLPHINS, WHO UNDULATE UP AND DOWN TO PROPEL THEMSELVES, ICHTHYOSAURS MOVED LEFT AND RIGHT JUST LIKE FISH. THOUGH THEY THRIVED DURING THE JURASSIC PERIOD, THE ICHTHYOSAURS LOST THEIR POSITION AT THE TOP OF THE FOOD CHAIN TO PLESIOSAURS IN THE CRETACEOUS PERIOD, AND WENT EXTINCT EVEN BEFORE DINOSAURS.

ICHTHYOSAURUS

AN ICHTHYOSAUR WHICH LIVED DURING THE JURASSIC PERIOD. APPROXIMATELY TWO METERS IN LENGTH.

PLESIOSAURUS

A PLESIOSAUR WHICH LIVED FROM THE LATE TRIASSIC TO THE EARLY JURASSIC. DUE TO THE PRESENCE OF GASTRALIA ("BELLY RIBS," ALSO FOUND IN TURTLES), THE PLESIOSAURUS LACKED FLEXIBILITY, AND COULD SCARCELY BEND ITS NECK IN ANY DIRECTION OTHER THAN DOWNWARD. IT IS ALSO BELIEVED THAT IT WAS NOT A VERY NIMBLE SWIMMER. THIS PARTICULAR SPECIES IS KNOWN TO HAVE GIVEN BIRTH TO LIVE YOUNG.

PTERANODON

A PTEROSAUR WHICH LIVED DURING THE LATE CRETACEOUS (BUT NOT AT THE SAME TIME AS TYRANNOSAURUS; SCENES DEPICTING THE TWO TOGETHER ARE NONSENSICAL). WHILE THEIR WINGSPANS COULD REACH BETWEEN SEVEN AND NINE METERS, THEY TYPICALLY WEIGHED ONLY FIFTEEN TO TWENTY KILOGRAMS. SINCE THERE WERE RELATIVELY FEW PLACES ON THEIR BODY WHERE THE MUSCLE NEEDED FOR WING-FLAPPING COULD HAVE BEEN ATTACHED, IT IS THOUGHT THAT THEY MOSTLY RELIED ON GLIDING.

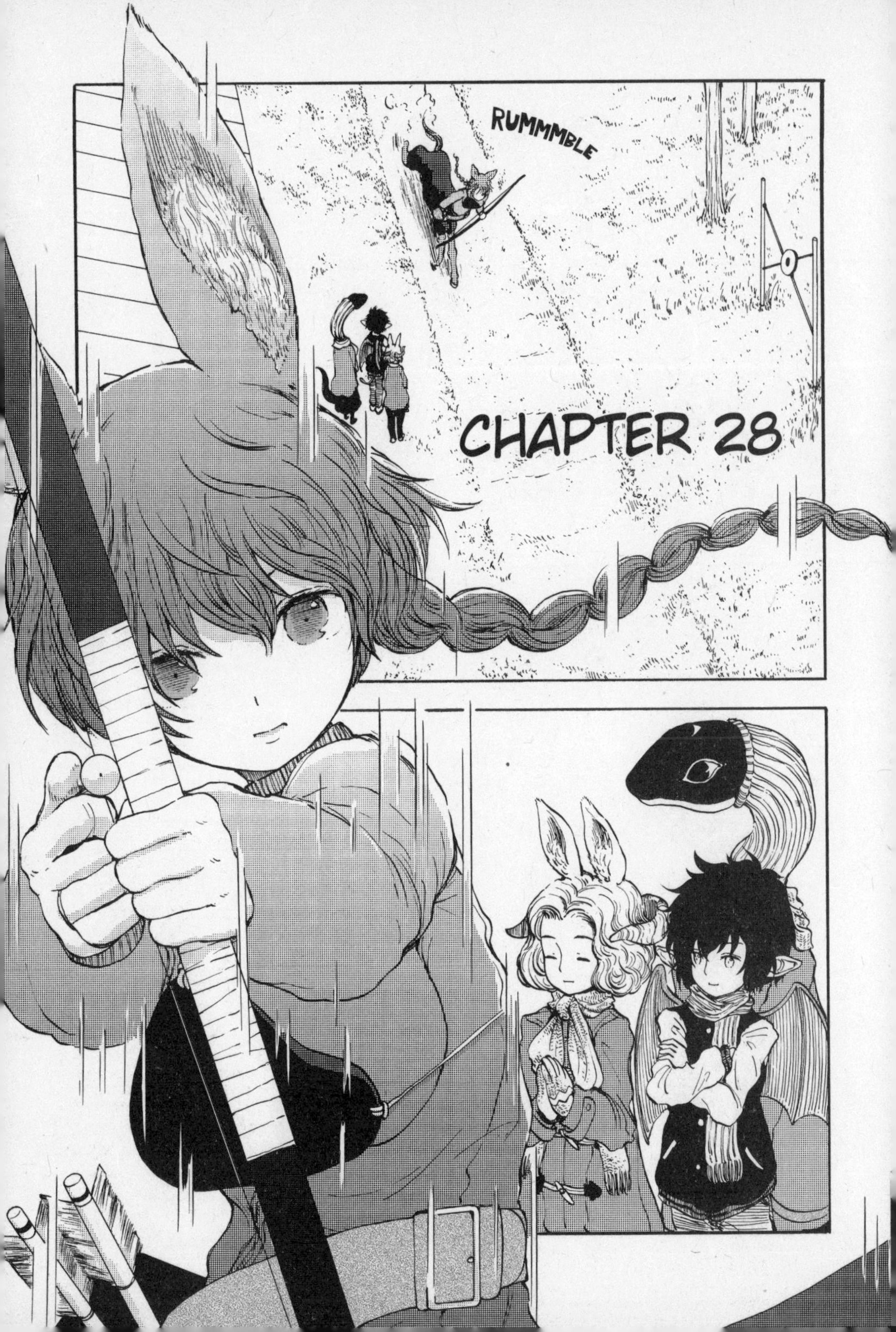
RUMMMBLE
CHAPTER 28

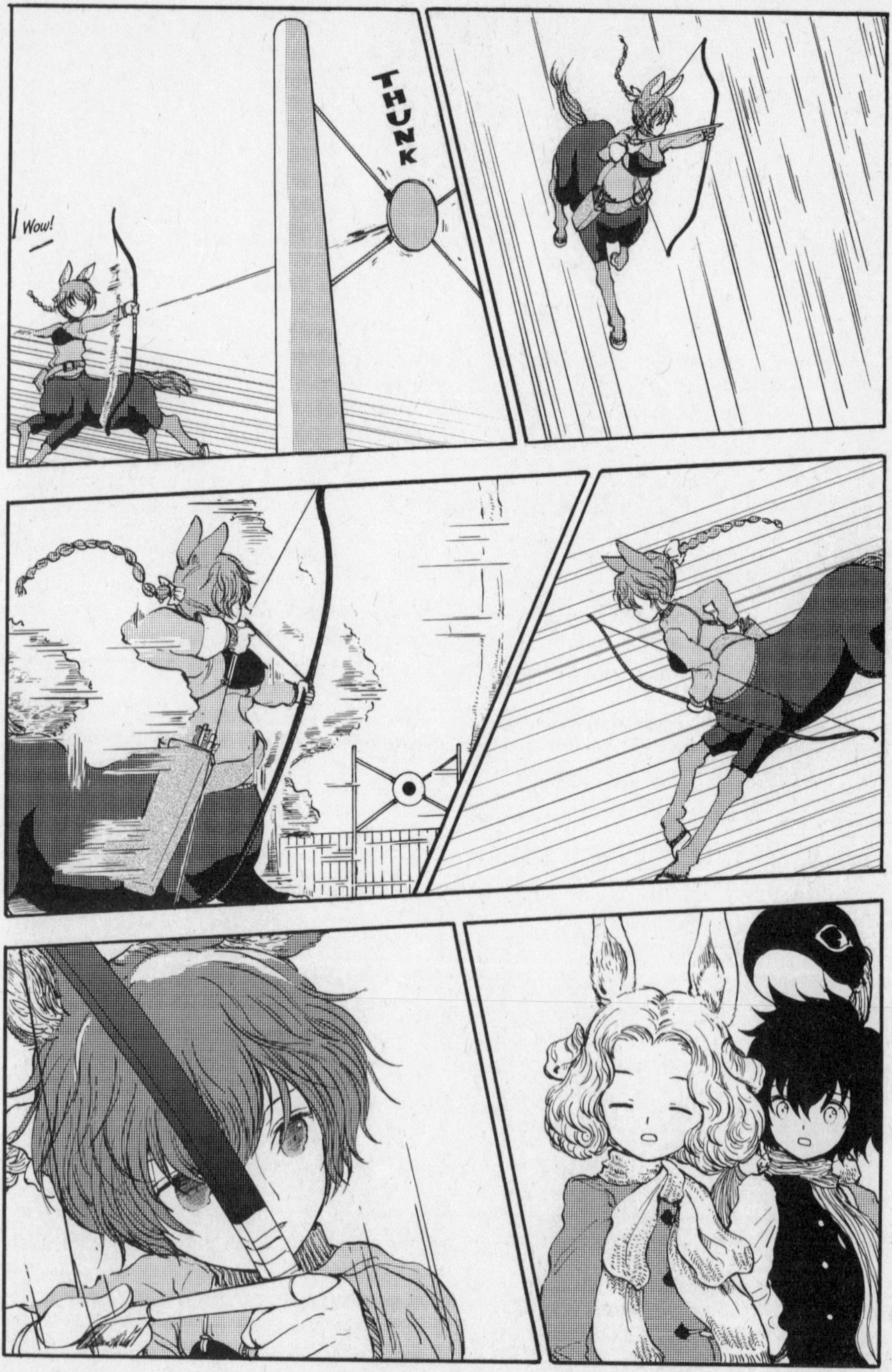
THUNK
Wow!

WOBBLE
Oh!
Ee-hee! ♡
What was that?!
SHWIP
YOU'RE GETTING LAZY, SENPAI!

SHWINK
EEP!
THUNK
Heh!
DON'T POINT ARROWS TOWARD PEOPLE! THAT'S DANGER-OUS!
FLAIL
FLAIL
UH, I-I'M SORRY...

HEY, WAIT A SEC!
THE POINT WAS TO SHOW THAT YOU'RE TOO LAID BACK!
I WAS TRYING TO PUT SOME **DISCIPLINE** INTO YOUR HEART!
UMM, HIME...?
OH...! THIS IS **WAKAMAKI AYAKA-CHAN.**
She's a middle school student, a year younger than us.
HELLO.

*Mounted archery.
**The Japanese martial art of archery.

PET PET

SHE'S VERY GOOD AT *YABUSAME*, AND EVEN *KYUDO*.

BUT SHE'S USUALLY VERY WELL-BEHAVED.

WHAT SHE DID WAS A BIT NAUGHTY...

YOU SAY I'M GOOD AT YABUSAME, SENPAI, BUT *YOU'RE* THE ONE WHO WON LAST YEAR!

PLEASE STOP THAT!

Ah!

Rebellious phase?!

BUT YOU WON'T WIN *THIS* YEAR!

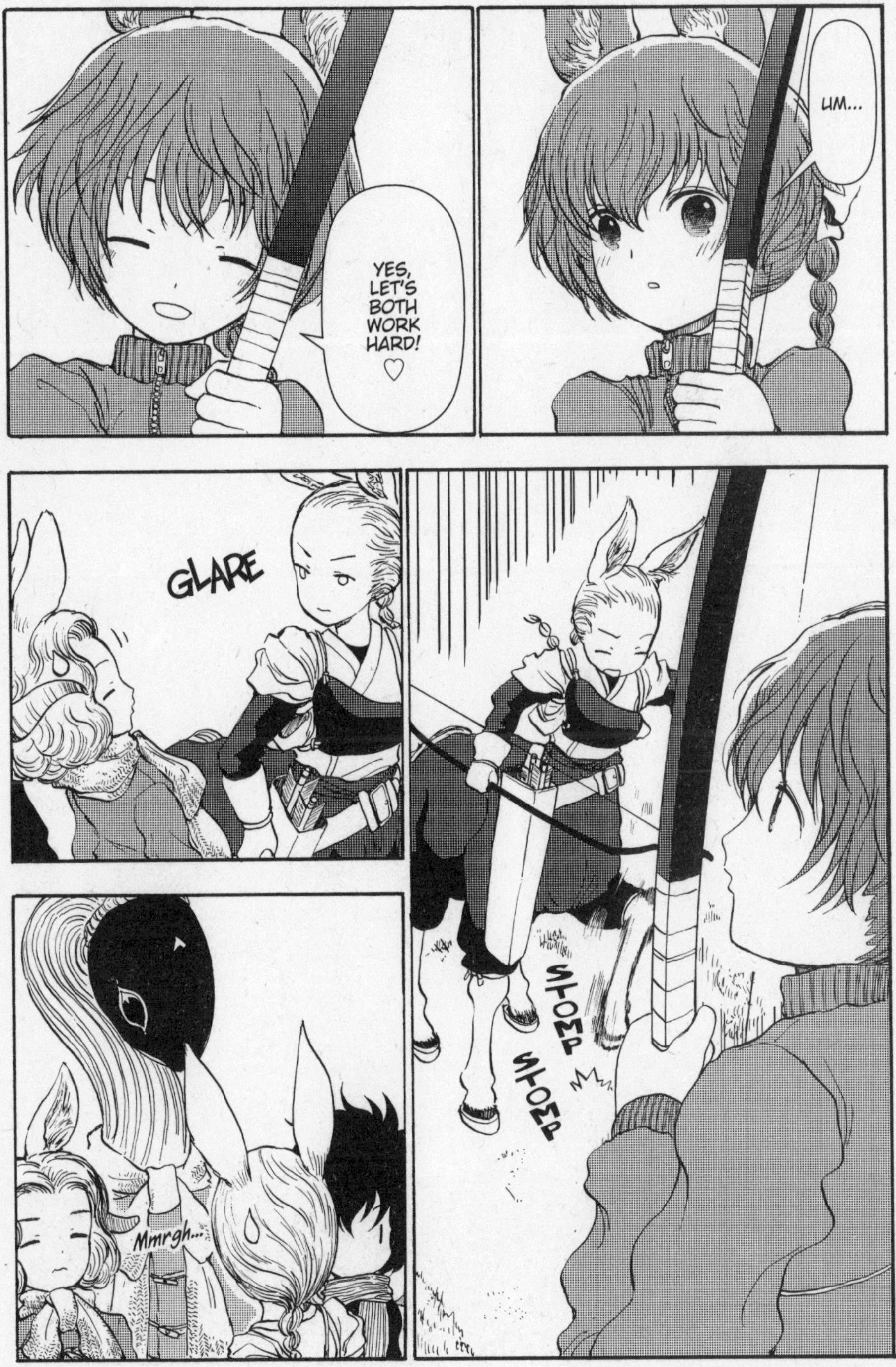

UM...
YES, LET'S BOTH WORK HARD! ♡
STOMP
STOMP
GLARE
Mmrgh...

Panel	Text
1	"I hope you can make her take this more seriously." "Farewell."
2	"I'm afraid you'll be *quite* disappointed." "If you're planning on cheering for senpai during this year's competition..."
3	"Ah...!"
4	"What is it?"
5	
6	"How was the kyudo tournament?"

We weren't even close in the team tournament.

I TOOK THIRD PLACE IN THE SINGLES TOURNAMENT AGAIN... NOT GOOD ENOUGH FOR NATIONALS.

SO TO MAKE GOOD MEMORIES OF MY MIDDLE SCHOOL YEARS...

I HAVE TO BEAT YOU AT YABUSAME, SENPAI!

POINT

JUST YOU WAIT!

CLIPPITY CLOP CLIPPITY CLOP

SHE'S A FEISTY ONE.

YEP...

THE COMPETITION BEFORE LAST DIDN'T GO WELL.

SHE MIGHT BE A LITTLE *TOO SERIOUS* ABOUT IT, THOUGH.

HEY, AYAKA-CHAN...
SO LAST YEAR, I TRIED SOME-THING TO HELP HER RELAX.
DID THAT HELP YOU RELAX?
BLAH~!
SMOOSH
Pfft?!
ARE YOU MOCKING ME?!

WOBBLE

FUME FUME

Ah---!!

Hee hee! Do it again! Do it again!

IT WORKS SO WELL WITH SHINO-CHAN.

SHE'S NOT A LITTLE KID.

NAH, IF SHE HATED YOU, SHE WOULDN'T HAVE TALKED TO YOU.

I THINK SHE HATES ME NOW.

ACTUALLY, I THINK SHE LIKES YOU...
A LOT. I'LL TELL YOU A GOOD WAY TO HANDLE AYAKA-CHAN.
DO YOU THINK THAT'LL BE OKAY?
IT'LL BE FINE. TRUST ME.
HEEEY.
THAT'S ENOUGH GIRL TALK. GET BACK TO WORK.
OKAY!
DO YOU GUYS WANT TO TRY KYUDO?

ESPECIALLY JAPANESE BOWS.

USING A BOW IS A LOT HARDER THAN IT LOOKS.

HUH?

BY THE WAY, WHY DID YOU DECIDE TO PICK UP ARCHERY, HIME-CHAN?

IF I DON'T, MY GRANDPA WILL COMPLAIN.

MY MOTHER TOLD ME TO DO IT.

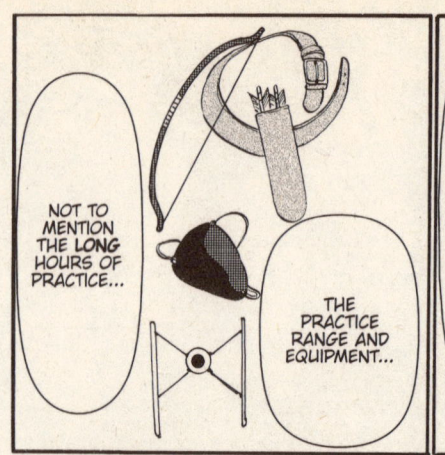

NOT TO MENTION THE LONG HOURS OF PRACTICE...

THE PRACTICE RANGE AND EQUIPMENT...

IT MAY BE DIFFERENT NOW, BUT IN THE PAST, THE COMPETITION...

IT'S MORE FOR FINDING A MARRIAGE PARTNER.

SO IT WAS FOR PROCREATION.

WELL, THAT IS A LITTLE TOO... DIRECT OF A DESCRIPTION.

IT WAS A GREAT PLACE FOR CENTAURS TO FIND OTHER CENTAURS TO MARRY TO THEIR SONS OR DAUGHTERS.

Quite nice.

THESE WERE ALL USED TO GAUGE A PERSON'S PHYSICAL AND MENTAL FITNESS.

She said "procreation."

DEPENDS ON THE TIME AND PLACE.

IS "PROCREATION" AN INAPPROPRIATE WORD? IT SEEMED ACCURATE...

UM, I'M NOT DOING IT TO... PROCREATE.
Really.
MAYBE YOU'LL GET MARRIED RIGHT AFTER HIGH SCHOOL.
NO. NO... PROBABLY NOT.
This is the 21st century.
BUT I WONDER ABOUT AYAKA-CHAN.
SHE'S FROM A PRETTY HIGH-CLASS FAMILY.
WELL, SHE'S NOT REALLY OLD ENOUGH TO GET MARRIED YET.
THERE ARE STILL FAMILIES THAT **DO** ARRANGED MARRIAGES, THOUGH.

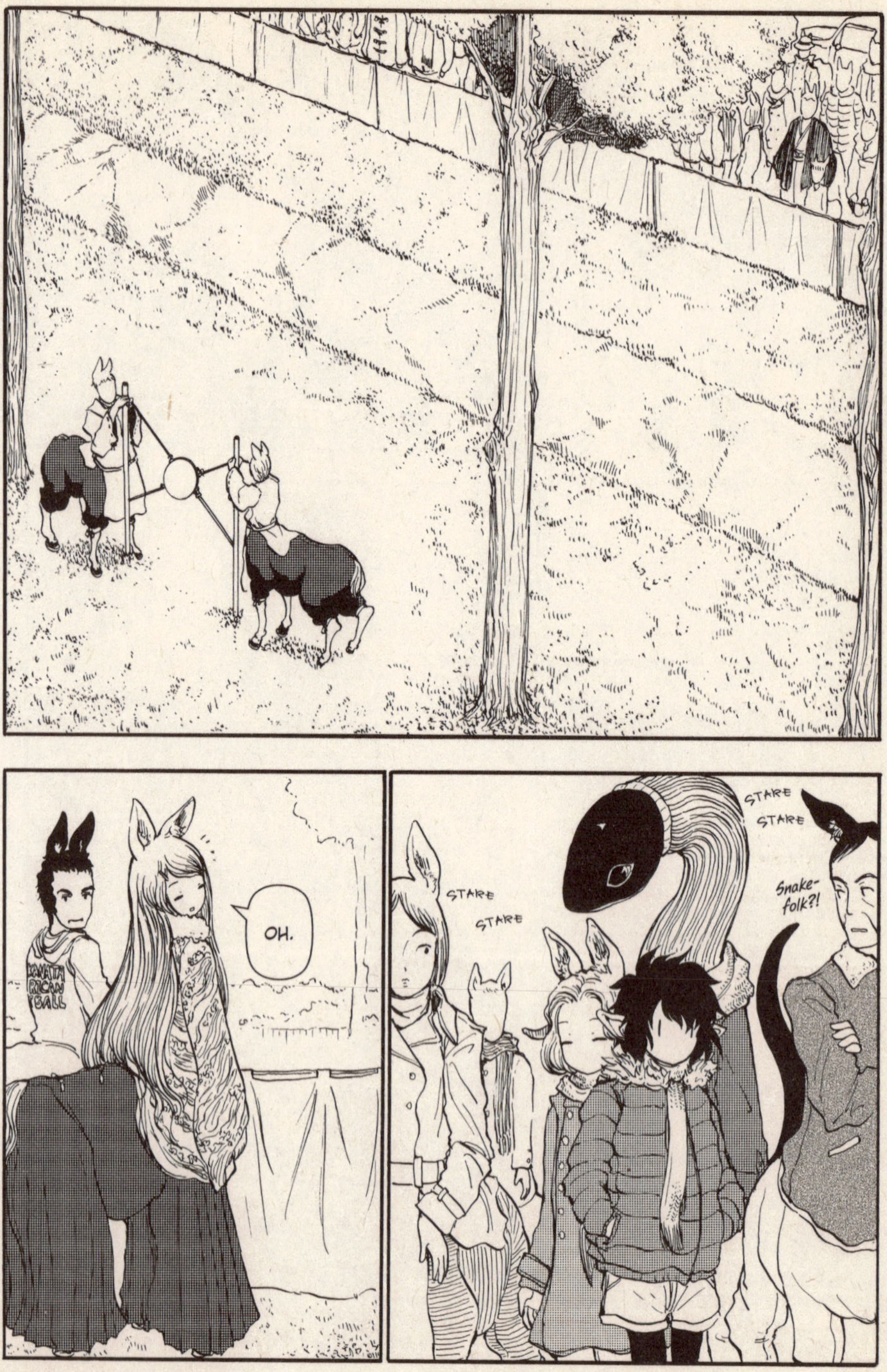
OH.
STARE
STARE
STARE
STARE
Snake-folk?!

HELLO.

I THINK THAT'S THE STUDENT COUNCIL VICE-PRESIDENT...

HI.

HELLO.

OH, HEY.

HELLO.

OH, SO THEY'RE UNDERCLASSMEN.

THEY'RE IN THE SAME CLASS AS KOMORI-KUN.

UM, WHO ARE THEY?

REMEMBER THAT STRIKING REDHEAD? I'M SURE THEY CAME TO WATCH HER COMPETE.

I see.

PLEASE ENJOY YOURSELVES.

OH, THEY'RE FRIENDS OF REI-CHAN.

Hey.
Hello ~!
Oh, hello.
What the heck...?
That was pretty normal.
NOZOMI-CHAN! KYO-CHAN! SUU-CHAN!
YOU LOOK SHARP TODAY.
HEE HEE.
Whoa, a snakefolk!
A dinosaur came?!

DO YOUR BEST~! BIG SIS, GOOD LUCK!	All contestants, please report to your designated places. WHOOPS, I GOTTA GO.

IT'S OKAY. BIG SIS IS RIGHT HERE. The dinosaur is scary!	Mmgh! WE CAN ALL CHEER FOR HER TOGETHER, TODAY.

No! We'll definitely take her---!

We won't take big sister Hime from you.

Come over here.

A GROWN MAN TALKING TO A HIGH SCHOOL GIRL?

WHY DON'T **YOU** GO TALK TO HER?

GO TALK TO HER FOR ME.

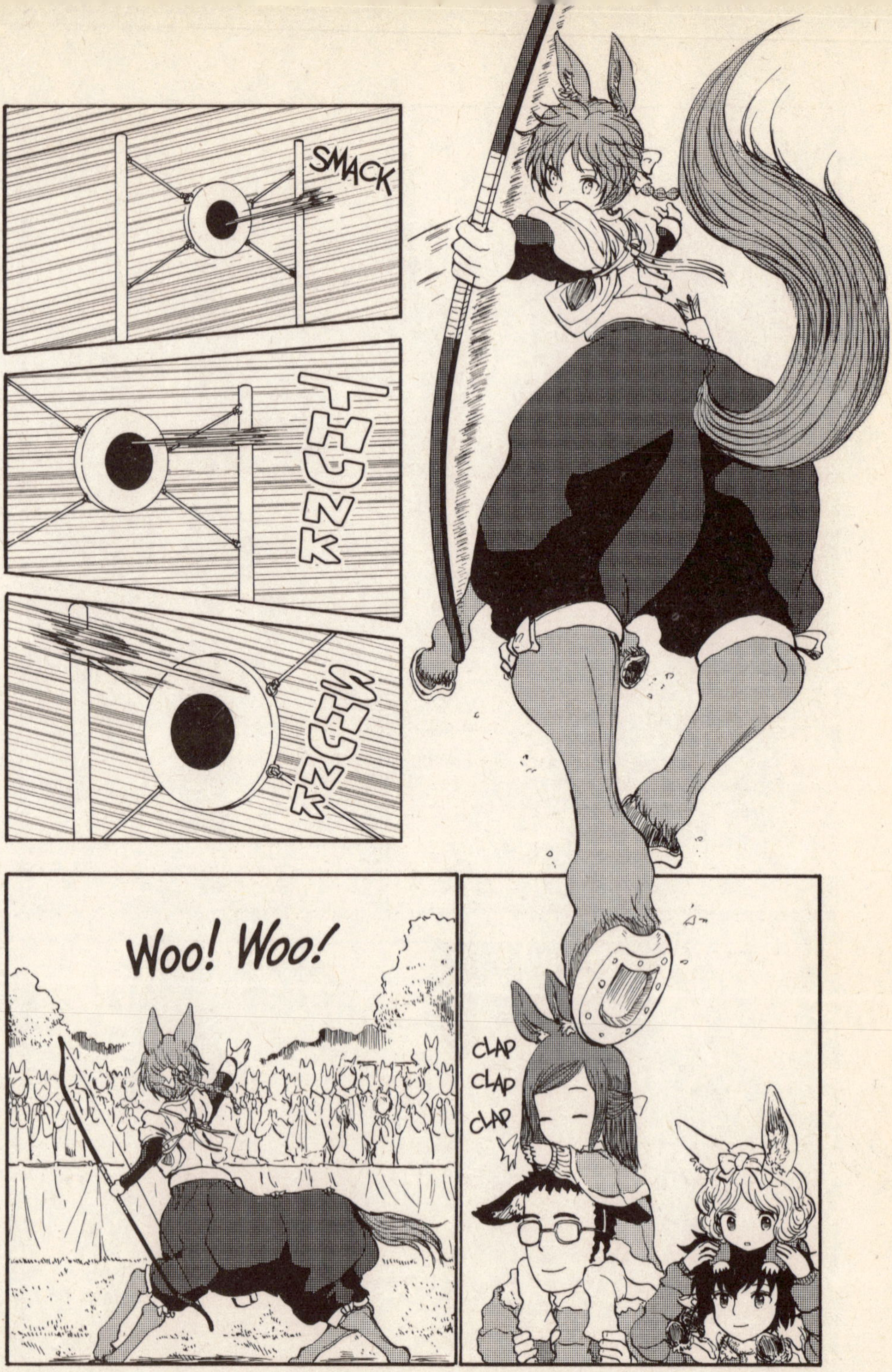
SMACK
THUNK
SHUNK
Woo! Woo!
CLAP
CLAP
CLAP

NICE JOB.
Next, Wakamaki Ayaka-san.
OH, THAT'S ME. GOTTA GO.
WAIT A SEC.
WHAT?! ARE YOU GOING TO SAY SOME-THING TO BREAK MY CONCEN-TRATION AGAIN?
NO.
LET'S MAKE A BET TO MAKE THINGS MORE EXCITING.
INTER-ESTING...
OKAY. IF I LOSE, I'LL DO WHATEVER YOU SAY.
THEN, IF I LOSE...
I'LL GO ON A DATE WITH YOU.

WH- WHAT ARE YOU...?!
I hope that was... okay?
Are you ready?
Always joking around like that! A "date"?!
Oh no! Where should we go?! What should I wear?!

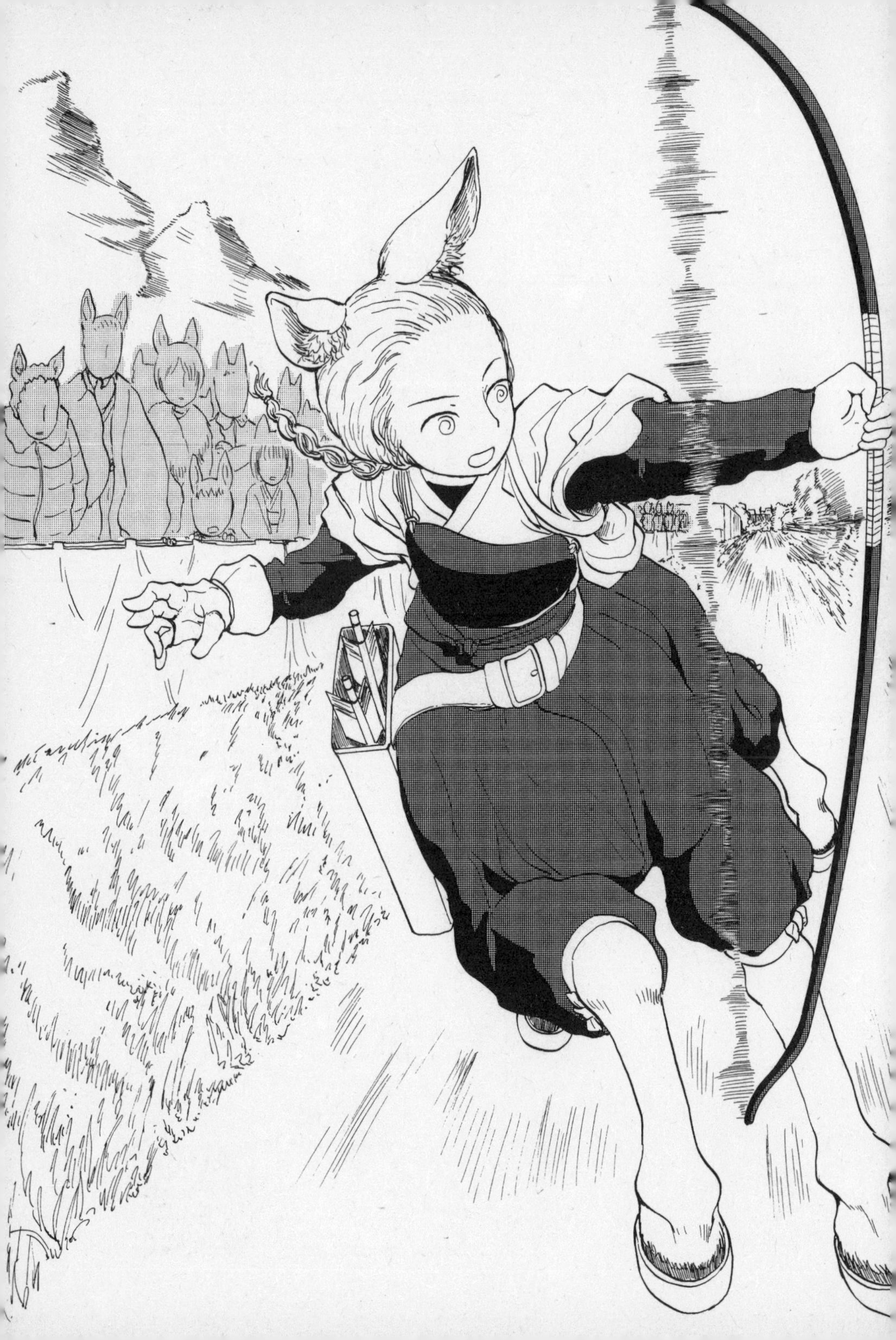

SORRY!
YOU'RE LATE, SENPAI.
WE HAVE A LOT OF PLACES TO GO.
Living and Fun
HUH?
SINCE YOU LOST, SENPAI, PLEASE JUST FOLLOW ME.
UM, OKAY!
Ah!
WHY ARE WE SPYING, AGAIN?
WHY NOT?

A Centaur's Life

MESOZOIC CREATURES

DINOSAURS AND THEIR CLOSE RELATIVES: IF DINOSAURS HADN'T GONE EXTINCT

IF DINOSAURS HADN'T GONE EXTINCT, WOULD MAMMALS EVER HAVE GONE ON TO PROSPER? THIS IS A TRICKY QUESTION. WHILE THE FOUR-SEASON CYCLE DID FIRST EMERGE DURING THE CRETACEOUS PERIOD, THE EARTH'S TEMPERATURE WAS STILL VERY HOT THROUGHOUT THE MESOZOIC ERA, PROVIDING A CLIMATE FOR WHICH THE DINOSAURS WERE VERY WELL SUITED.

HOWEVER, THE EARTH IS A GREAT DEAL COOLER THAN IT WAS THEN, AND IT'S BEEN VISITED BY A NUMBER OF ICE AGES IN THE MEANTIME. IT'S LIKELY THEY WOULD HAVE GONE EXTINCT ANYWAY, UNABLE TO COPE WITH THE EARTH'S COOLING CLIMATE, OR ELSE VASTLY DECREASED IN NUMBER, ALLOWING MAMMALS TO FLOURISH. ALTERNATIVELY, THEY MIGHT HAVE ADAPTED TO THE COLD TEMPERATURES, THEREBY KEEPING MAMMALS SHOVED OFF INTO AN ECOLOGICAL NICHE FOR SMALL CREATURES. ONE CAN ALSO IMAGINE THAT THEY MIGHT HAVE EVOLVED INTO INTELLECTUAL LIFE FORMS A LA THE SNAKEFOLK AND MERFOLK AND COME TO COEXIST WITH HUMANKIND.

LET'S IMAGINE NOW WHAT IT WOULD HAVE BEEN LIKE IF DINOSAURS HAD INDEED EVOLVED LIKE HUMANS RATHER THAN GOING EXTINCT.

DINOSAURFOLK

A WIDELY POPULAR MODEL USED BEFORE THE DISCOVERY OF THE ANTARCTICAN SNAKEFOLK. IT SHOWS THE THEORY THAT, JUST AS THE REPTILIAN ICHTHYOSAURS HAD EVOLVED TO RESEMBLE FISH SPECIES AND DOLPHINS, SO TOO COULD SPECIES HAVE COME TO RESEMBLE HUMAN BEINGS IF THEY WERE TO EVOLVE IN SIMILAR WAYS. NOTABLY, THIS MODEL, DEPICTING THE FIGURE OF A YOUNG, FOUR-ARMED GIRL, IS THE ONLY ONE ON DISPLAY AT THE SHIMODA JAPAN NATURAL HISTORY MUSEUM. WHILE A BROADER VARIETY OF FIGURES--MALE AND FEMALE, YOUNG AND OLD--HAD ORIGINALLY BEEN PLANNED, A CHANGE IN GOVERNMENT ADMINISTRATION RESULTED IN THE PROJECT'S FUNDING BEING PULLED. ONLY THIS FIGURE, WHICH WAS ALREADY IN PRODUCTION, WAS SEEN TO COMPLETION--ALBEIT AT THE PROJECT SUPERVISOR'S OWN PERSONAL EXPENSE.

FURTHERMORE, THE FIGURE WAS ORIGINALLY DISPLAYED IN THE NUDE, BUT DUE TO THE REGRETTABLE HUMAN INABILITY TO MAINTAIN SCHOLARLY COMPOSURE, THE PROJECT SUPERVISOR AND CREATOR DECIDED TO ADORN IT WITH CLOTHES FROM HIS HOME. DUE TO THESE EVENTS, THERE HAVE BEEN SCATTERED ALLEGATIONS ON THE NET THAT THE CREATOR PROJECTED HIS OWN PERSONAL TASTES ONTO THE MODEL, BUT THESE CLAIMS ARE COMPLETELY GROUNDLESS.

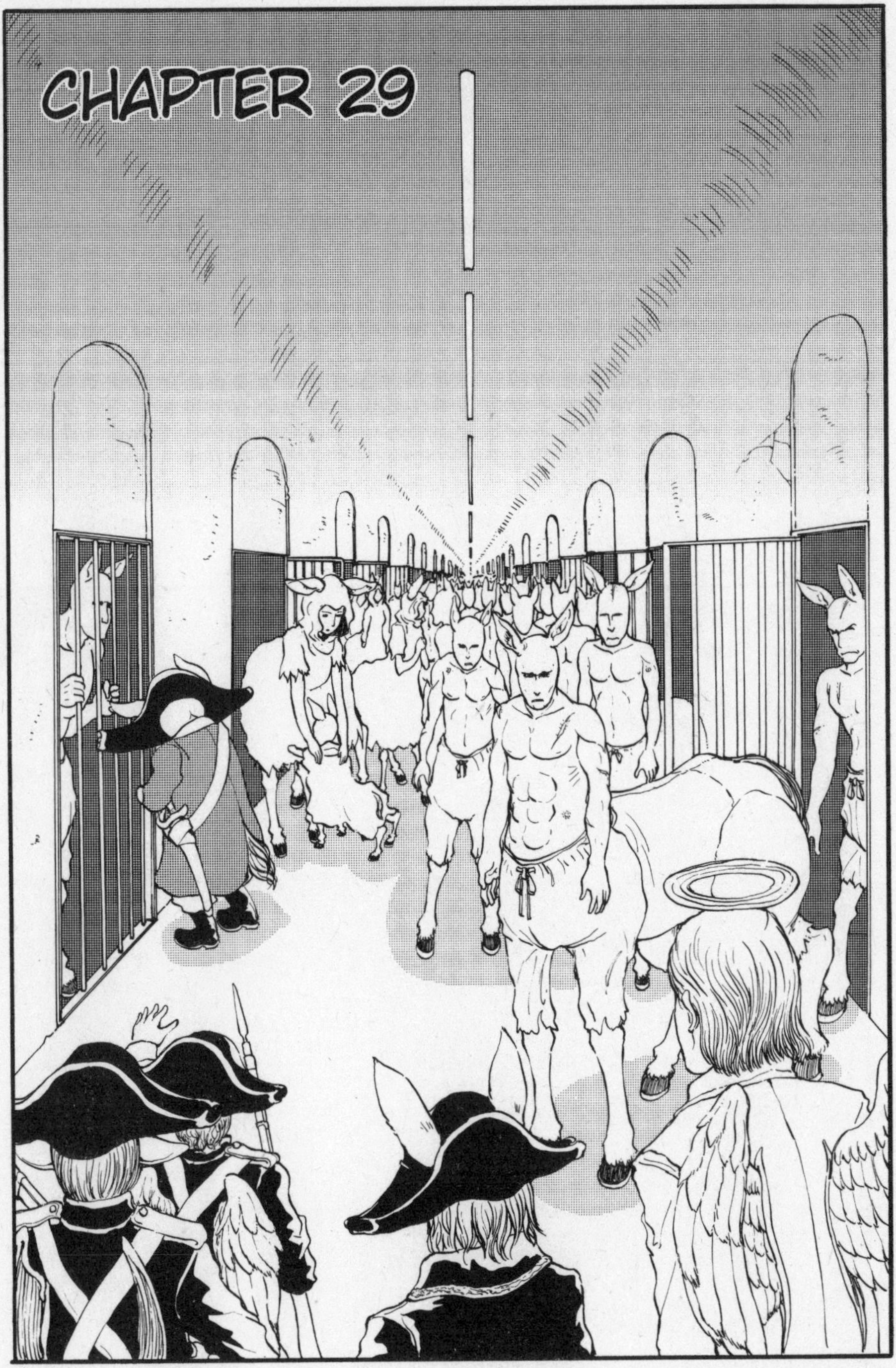
CHAPTER 29

CENTAURS!

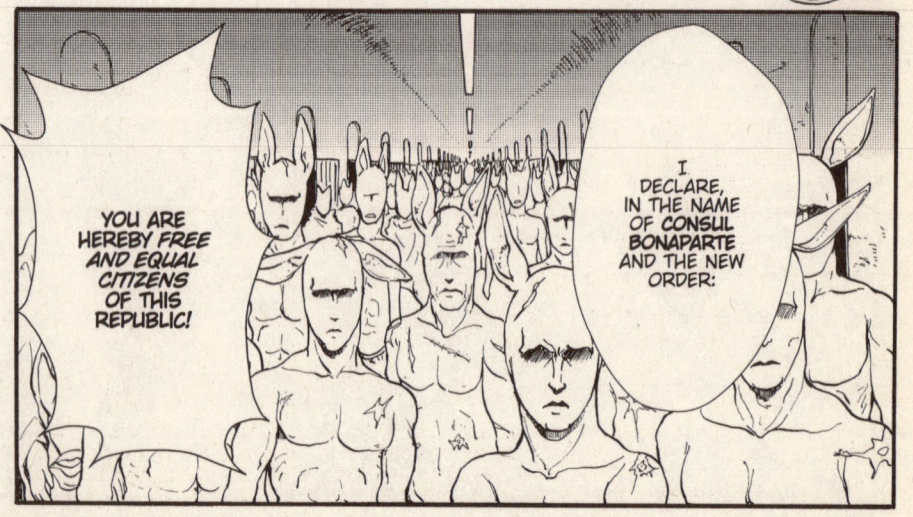

YOU ARE NO LONGER SLAVES! YOU HAVE BEEN FREED!

I DECLARE, IN THE NAME OF CONSUL BONAPARTE AND THE NEW ORDER:

YOU ARE HEREBY *FREE AND EQUAL CITIZENS* OF THIS REPUBLIC!

SILENCE
GLANCE
I SAY. THEY DO UNDER-STAND OUR LANGUAGE, DON'T THEY?
YES. THEY HIDE IT, THOUGH, BECAUSE THEY WOULD'VE BEEN PUNISHED FOR IT BEFORE NOW.
LONG LIVE THE REVOLU-TION!
LONG LIVE THE REPUBLIC!

ARE WE TRULY FREED?
YOU ARE INDEED!
LONG LIVE FREE-DOM!
LONG LIVE EQUAL-ITY!
HURRAH
VIVE!!
LONG LIVE FREEDOM!
LONG LIVE BONAPARTE!

HEH HEH. THEY SEEM RATHER PLEASED, NO?
BUT THEIR TROUBLES ARE JUST BEGINNING.
THEY WHO HAVE KNOWN NOTHING BUT SLAVERY HAVE NO FOUNDATION UPON WHICH TO START LIVES OF THEIR OWN.
IF THEY'RE LEFT TO THEIR OWN DEVICES, IT WILL LEAD TO SOCIAL UNREST.
IT IS OF GREAT URGENCY THAT THEY ARE GIVEN JOBS AND HOMES, ALONG WITH--
FEAR NOT!
JOBS AND HOMES ALIKE HAVE BEEN MADE TO ORDER!

KA-BOOM
KA-BOOM
BUDDA
BUDDA
BUDDA
BUDDA
BUDDA
BUDDA
KRAKOW
KRAKOW
KA-BOOM
ROAAAARRR
KRAKOW
K-SHNK
K-SHNK

MEN!
KA-BOOM
YES, THE VERY REPUBLIC WHICH BROUGHT YOU *LIBERTY* AND *EQUALITY!*
CALAMITY ENCROACHES UPON OUR FATHER-LAND!

IT NOW STANDS TO BE TRAMPED DOWN BY THE VERY MONARCHS, NOBLES, AND KNAVES WHO ONCE OPPRESSED YOU!

SHMP

KA-BOOM

KAPOW KAPOW

FIGHT! TO PROTECT YOUR LIBERTY AND EQUALITY!

CLIPPITY CLOP CLIPPITY CLOP

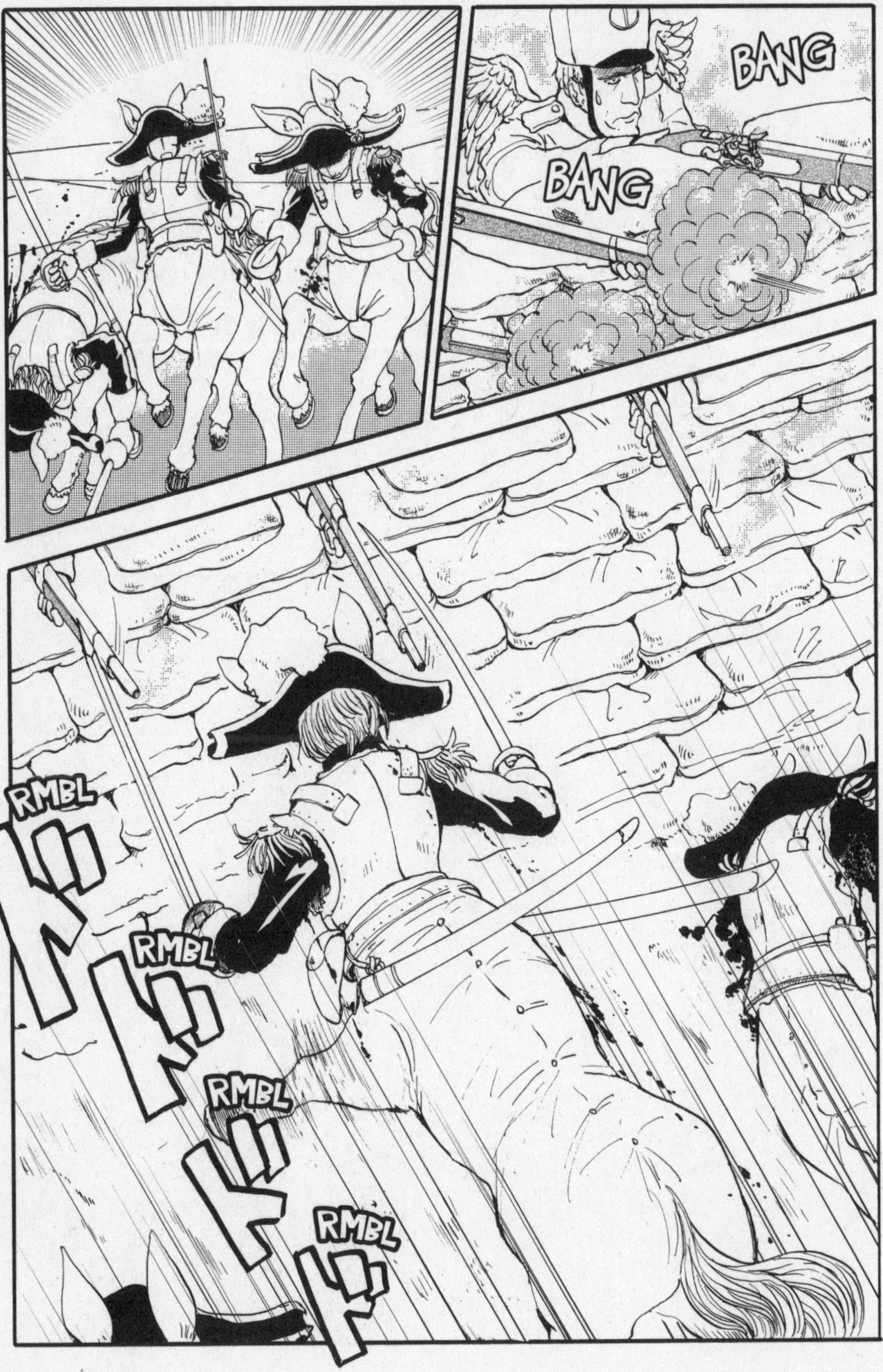
BANG
BANG
RMBL
RMBL
RMBL
RMBL

KILL THE *FOES* OF OUR FATHERLAND!
KILL THEM!
KILL THOSE WHO STAND AGAINST *FREEDOM, EQUALITY, AND BROTHERHOOD!*

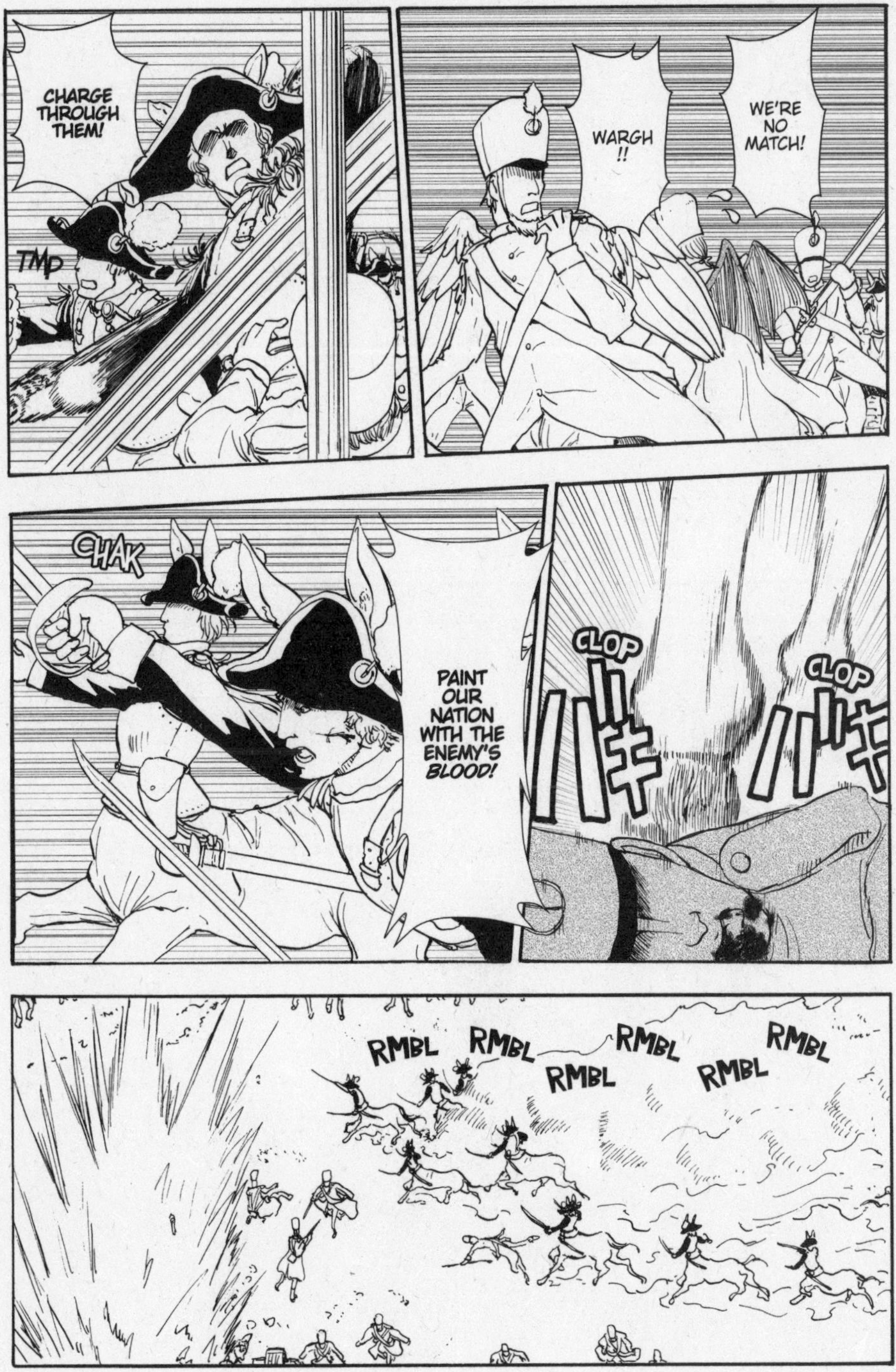
WE'RE NO MATCH!
WARGH !!
CHARGE THROUGH THEM!
TMP
CLOP
バキ
CLOP
バキ
PAINT OUR NATION WITH THE ENEMY'S *BLOOD!*
CHAK
RMBL
RMBL
RMBL
RMBL
RMBL
RMBL

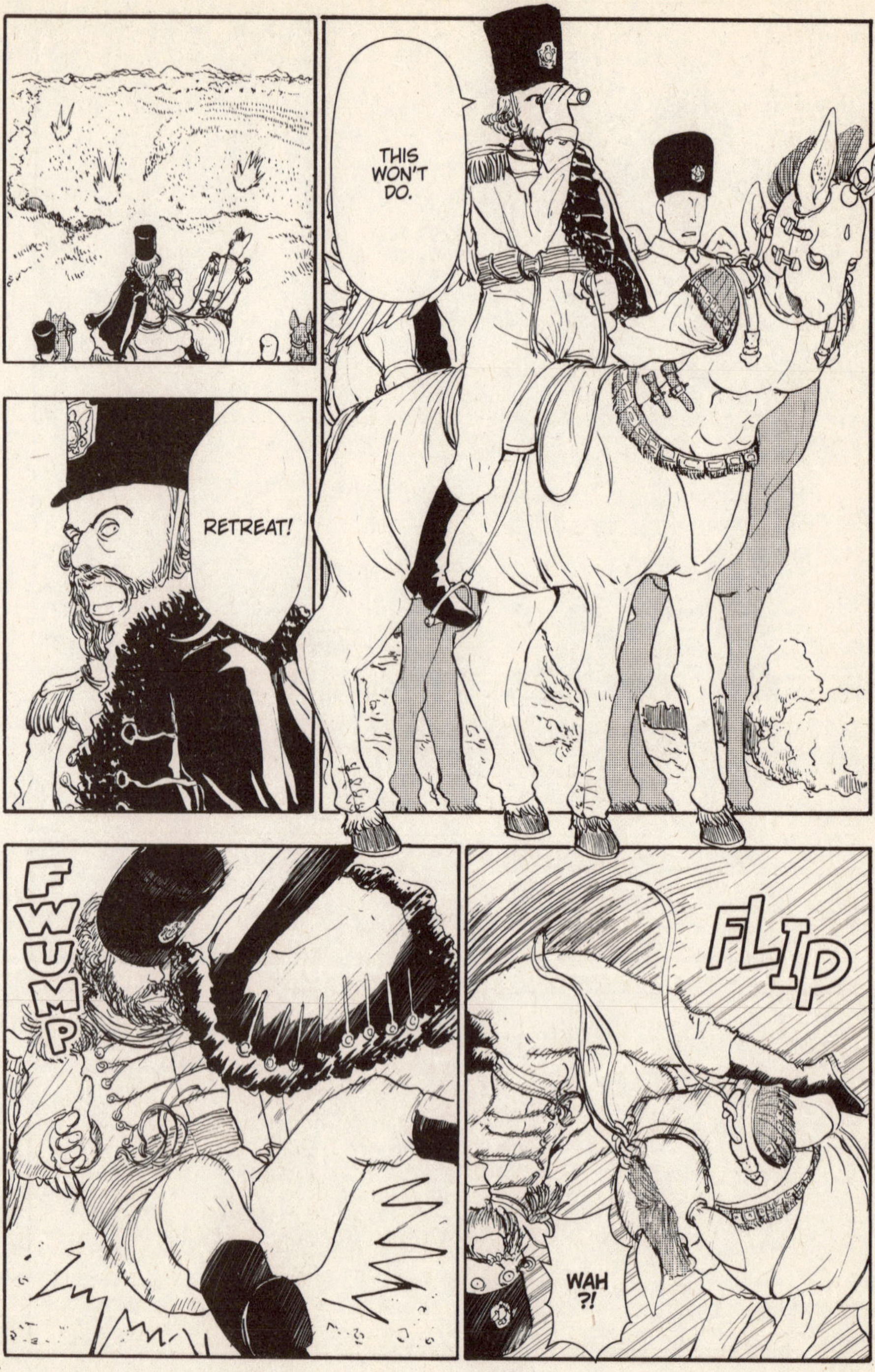
THIS WON'T DO.
RETREAT!
FWUMP
FLIP
WAH ?!

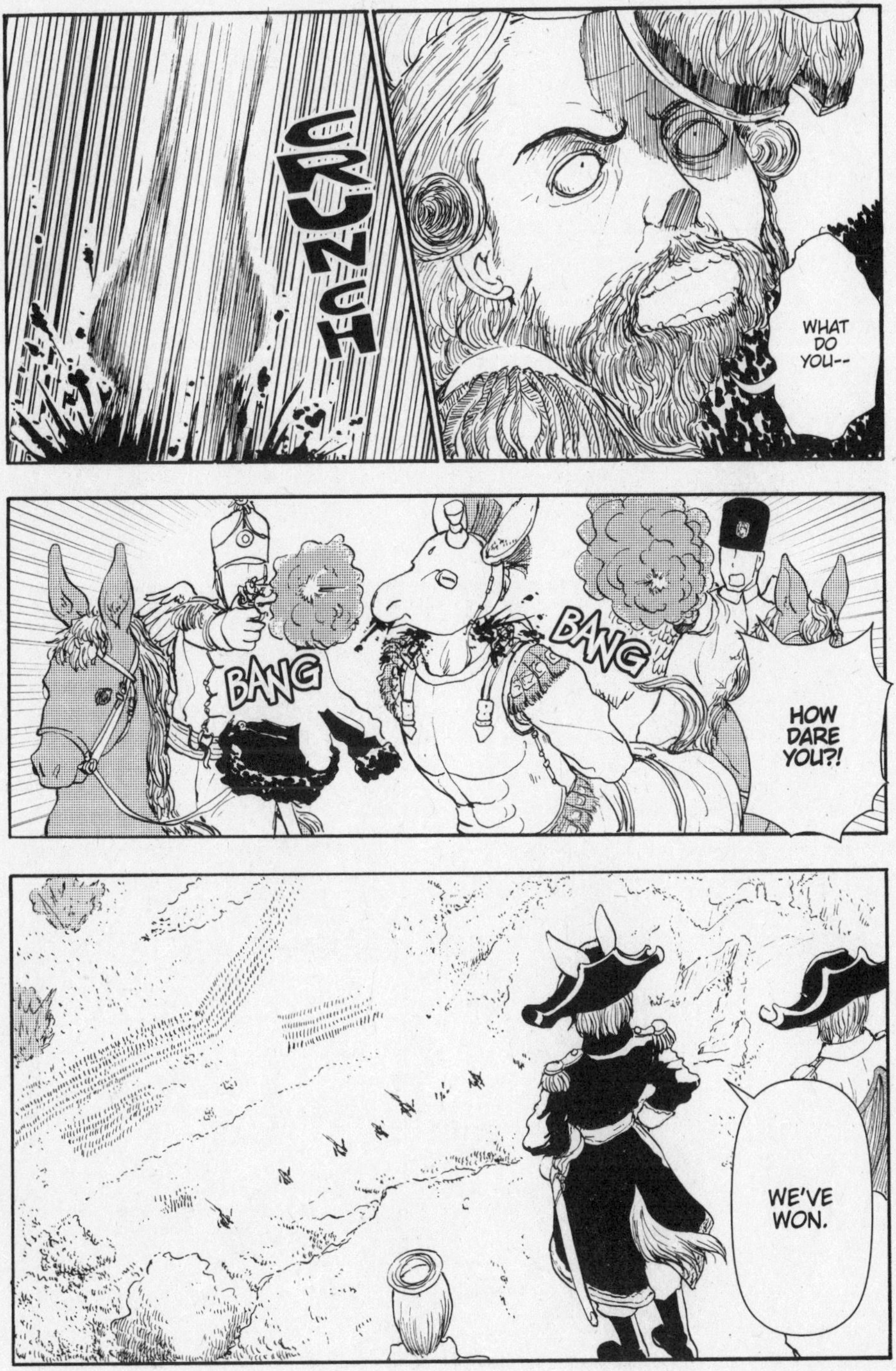

CRUNCH
WHAT DO YOU--
BANG
BANG
HOW DARE YOU?!
WE'VE WON.

SEEK OUT ANY CENTAUR SLAVES WHO ARE CAPABLE OF UNDER-STANDING SPEECH.

SIRE?

AND ONCE FOUND, SIRE?
THEY'RE AT RISK OF GETTING RILED UP BY FOREIGN REVOLUTIONARIES AND REVOLTING.
KILL THEM.
NEARLY ALL CENTAURS UNDERSTAND SPEECH.
THEY MERELY HIDE IT TO AVOID PUNISHMENT.
S-SIRE, SURELY WE NEEDN'T KILL THEM...
WE'VE SPENT A GREAT DEAL OF MONEY RAISING AND CARING FOR THEM.
IF WE SIMPLY OFFERED THEM A BIT BETTER FOOD AND BEDS TO SLEEP IN--
IT'S TOO LATE FOR THAT!
I DON'T CARE IF YOU HAVE TO KILL EVERY LAST ONE OF THEM! DO IT!

EEP!

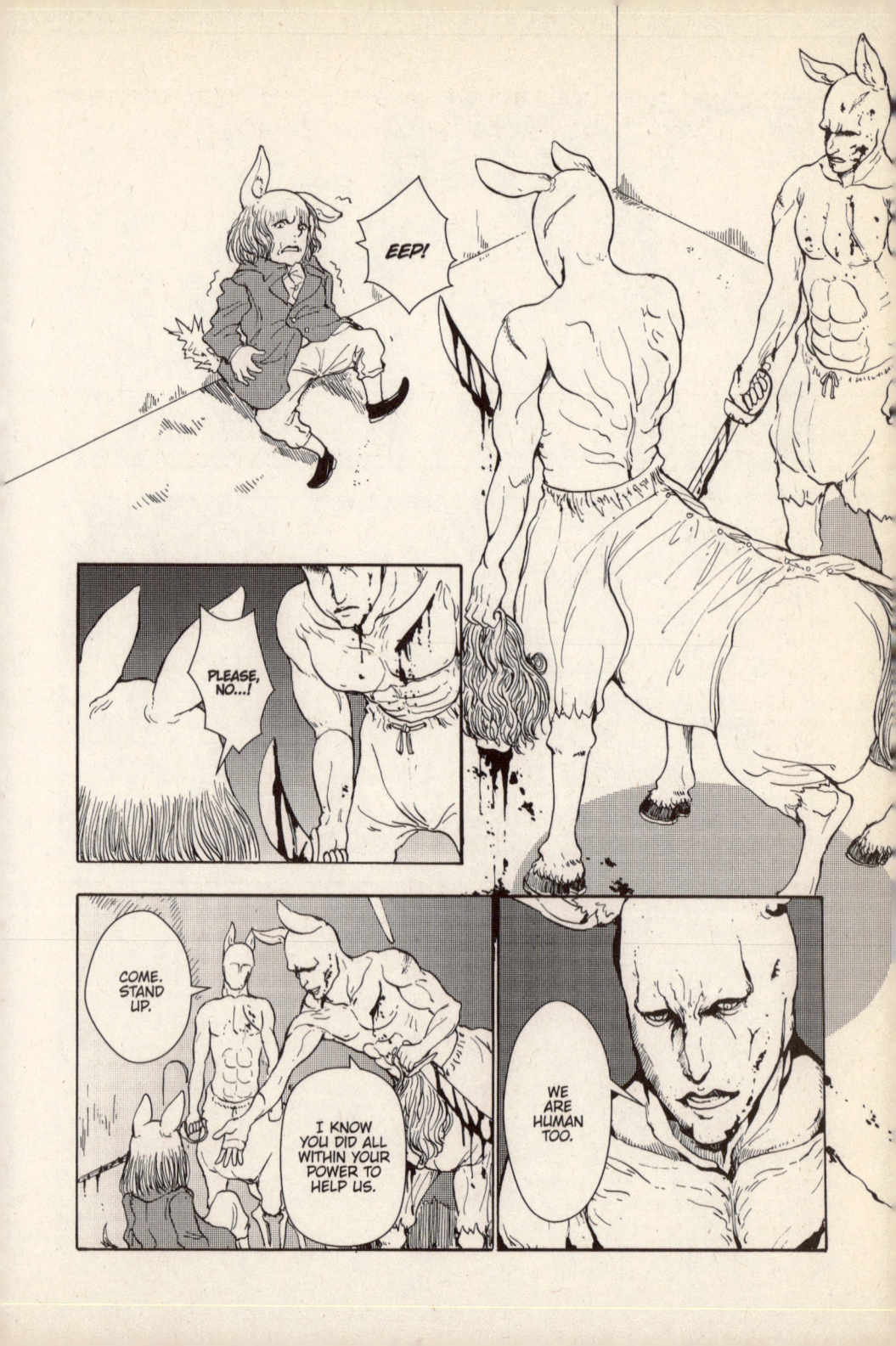

PLEASE, NO...!

COME. STAND UP.

I KNOW YOU DID ALL WITHIN YOUR POWER TO HELP US.

WE ARE HUMAN TOO.

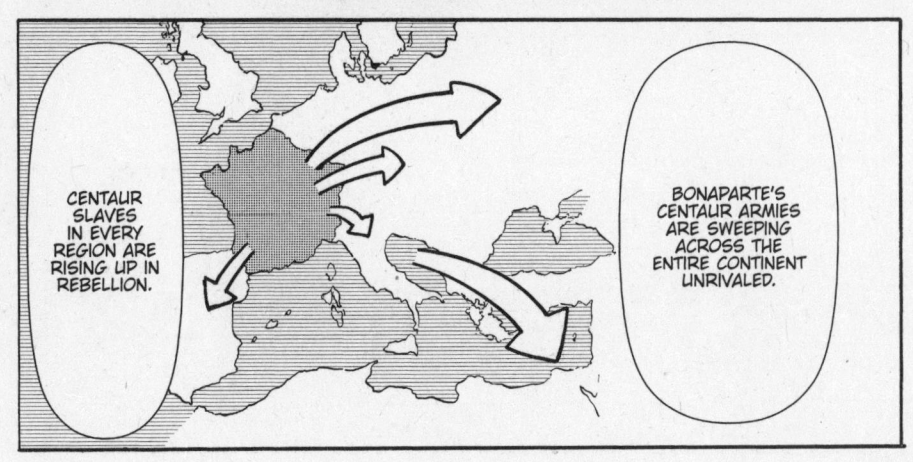

LIBERATING THE CENTAURS IS *OUT OF THE QUESTION!*

SO WHAT IF THEY ARE FILTHY?

LOOK AT THE REALITY OF THE SITUATION.

WE'RE NOT SOME BACKWARD COUNTRY! YOU'RE SUGGESTING WE TREAT THOSE *FILTHY CENTAURS* LIKE *HUMAN BEINGS?!*

CENTAUR SLAVES IN EVERY REGION ARE RISING UP IN REBELLION.

BONAPARTE'S CENTAUR ARMIES ARE SWEEPING ACROSS THE ENTIRE CONTINENT UNRIVALED.

IT'S ONLY A MATTER OF TIME BEFORE THEY INVADE THIS NATION AS WELL.
WE HAVE DOMINANT FLEETS AND BRILLIANT ADMIRALS ON OUR SIDE!
THAT MAY PREVENT AN OUTSIDE INVASION, BUT WHAT ABOUT ONE FROM WITHIN?
WE'LL SIMPLY SLAUGHTER **ALL** CENTAURS IN THE NATION!
UTTER FOOLISHNESS.
THAT WOULD MERELY *FORCE* THEM TO REVOLT.
AND I TRUST THAT LITTLE MAN BONAPARTE WILL OFFER THE REBELS PLENTY OF SUPPORT.

IT'D BE NO SURPRISE IF WE WOUND UP WITH OUR HEADS NEXT TO OUR KING'S, ALL LINED UP IN FRONT OF HIM!
GULP
HOWEVER, IF WE INSTEAD LIBERATE THE NATION'S CENTAURS PREEMPTIVELY,
THEY SHALL BECOME A POWERFUL WEAPON WE CAN USE TO **STRIKE BACK** AT BONAPARTE.
HA! IT SEEMS THE POMPOUS ASSES HAVE FINALLY GRASPED THE REALITY OF THE SITUATION.
HM. WE SHALL FIND OURSELVES QUITE BUSY SOON ENOUGH.
I WANT YOU TO BRING TOGETHER YOUR COMPATRIOTS.
YES, MY LORD.

"ANYTHING INTERESTING IN THE NEWS?"

"MORE WARRING BETWEEN SPECIES IN THE BAGARA KINGDOM."

"INDEED."

"UTTER BARBARIANS."

A Centaur's Life

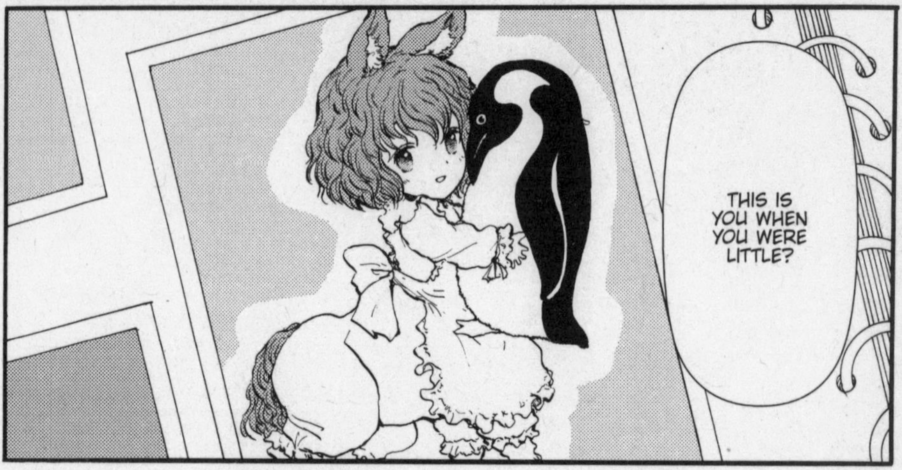
THIS IS YOU WHEN YOU WERE LITTLE?

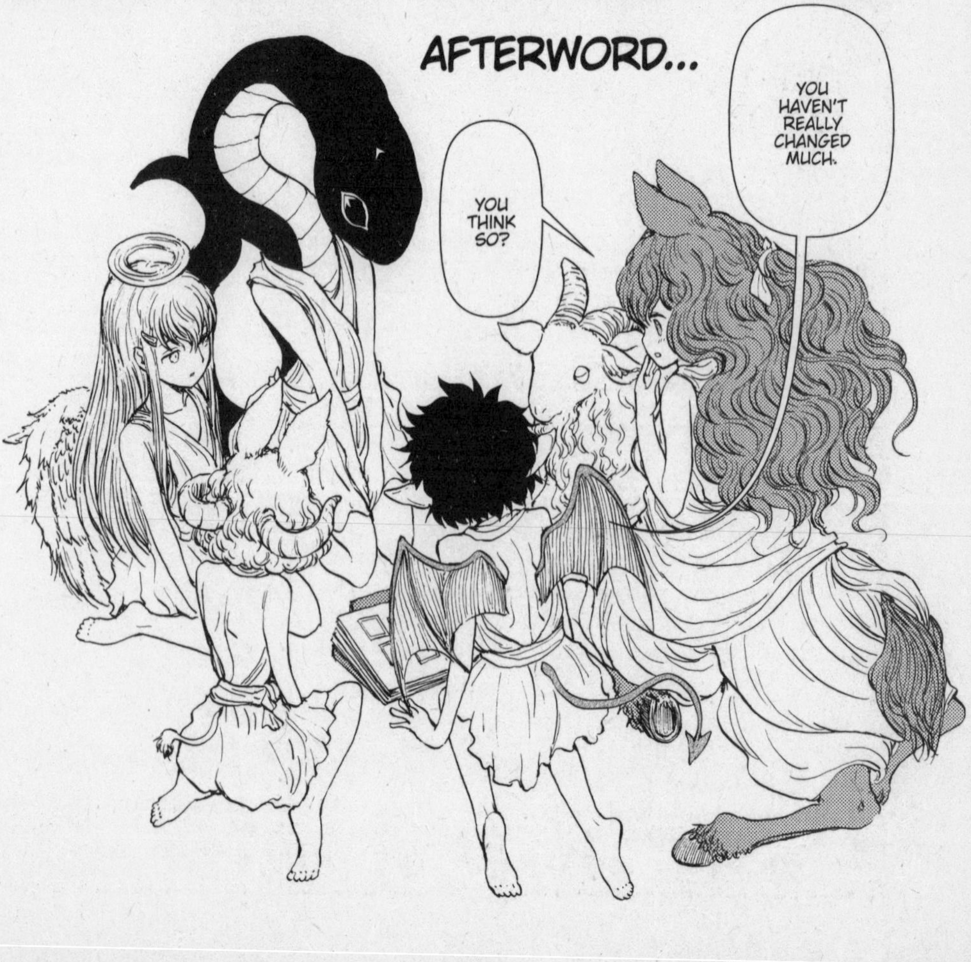
AFTERWORD...
YOU HAVEN'T REALLY CHANGED MUCH.
YOU THINK SO?

WHAT WERE YOU LIKE, NOZOMI-CHAN?
Let me guess... you used to be soft-spoken, or something.
NAH, SHE'S ALWAYS BEEN LIKE SHE IS NOW.
SHE'S EXACTLY THE SAME.
SHUT UP!
WHAT ABOUT KYO-CHAN?
SHE'S NO DIFFERENT, EITHER.
ALL I HAVE TO GO BY ARE WRITTEN SYMBOLS.
YEP, NO HELP THERE.
LOOKS LIKE THE PREZ HERE HAS CHANGED THE MOST.
IT'S LIKE... MAN, YOU'VE BEEN THROUGH A LOT.
You were identical to Sue-chan.
WH-WHAT DO YOU MEAN...?

THE GROWTH OF KANATA
THROUGH INDUSTRY AND WATER TRANSPORTATION

During the Kamikura and Muromachi eras, the Oda family made Oda castle (the Oda district in modern Kanata City) the seat of government power. Oda castle was built on tableland between Mount Houkyou* and the wetlands nearby that have become rice fields in modern times. This location was not considered militarily strategic, unlike the locations of other castles. So why would the Oda family, governors of the Hidachi prefecture, choose such a place?

The answer is that the castle was adjacent to the Sanzuse River (also known as the Ake River). This river not only opened to a large inland sea, called the Katori Sea, but to the rest of the nation for water transport and shipping. The Katori Sea runs between what is currently Kasumigaura and Teganuma/Inbanuma, connecting them together. It serves as a junction for several smaller rivers-- for instance, you can reach the bay of the Imperial City through the old Tonegawa water system.

During these eras, centaurs were still used as the primary form of transportation. River traffic, however, allowed for the movement of troops and supplies in greater volumes, thus cementing its place as a lifeline for the leaders of the time.

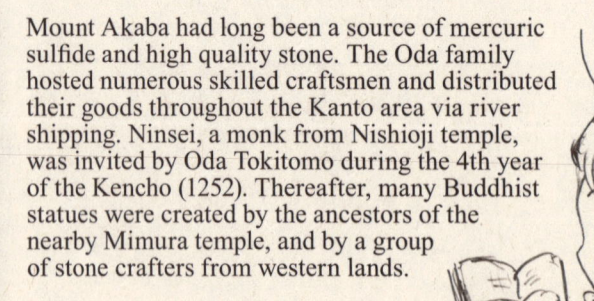

Mount Akaba had long been a source of mercuric sulfide and high quality stone. The Oda family hosted numerous skilled craftsmen and distributed their goods throughout the Kanto area via river shipping. Ninsei, a monk from Nishioji temple, was invited by Oda Tokitomo during the 4th year of the Kencho (1252). Thereafter, many Buddhist statues were created by the ancestors of the nearby Mimura temple, and by a group of stone crafters from western lands.

Remains of a Five Ringed Tower at Gokuraku Temple on Mount Houkyou

*Originally called Mount Mimura, but renamed Mount Houkyou after the Houkyou tower was built at its peak. It is also locally called Mount Oda. It was once the site of many monasteries and convents, but most have been long abandoned.

THE CONFLICT AND TENSION BETWEEN THE HOUJOU FAMILY'S INFLUENCE AND HIDACHI'S GOVERNOR

After the death of En no Yoritomo and the establishment of the Kamikura shogunate, After the death of En no Yoritomo and the establishment of the Kamikura shogunate, Yada no Tomoie (ancestor of the Oda family--his son Tomoshige changed the family name back to Oda) was one of the thirteen council members that assisted the second generation shogun, Yoriie, to govern the shogunate.

The governorship of Hidachi had been passed down within the Oda family for generations, but the Houjou family received that power after the shogun line of the En family ended in just three generations. During the Rebellion of Shokyu between the Kamikura shogunate and the Emperor Gouba, the Houjou family not only survived the Mongol attack, but eliminated powerful families of the shogunate, such as Miura and Adachi Yasumori, gaining power that even affected Hidachi. Thus, during the first year of Bunpo (1317), the governor's seat was given not to a member of the Oda family, but to Sasuke no Tokitsuna, a member of the Houjou family.

Here, we will explain a little of the Kamikura shogunate. It is often misunderstood, but the establishment of the Kamikura shogunate did not mean that the preexisting government and aristocracy were destroyed in a single night. The provincial governors and Kokuga** of various provinces coexisted for quite some time. The Kamikura Bakufu held two important administrative duties. First of all, it could appoint *Jito,* or lords, responsible for operating the manors peppered across the land. Secondly, it presided over the governors in each state responsible for oversight of the military, police, and the aforementioned regional *Jito*. Their authority initially only extended to vassals (military retainers to the Bakufu) in the eastern region. At first, the Bakufu's influence was limited only to governance of the samurai in the east. However, as a result of the Bakufu's victory in the Joukyuu Rebellion, their advantage over the imperial court became solidified, and their influence spread westward as they commanded a defense against the Mongols. Meanwhile, the *Jito* and governors began exercising their newfound authority to seize manors, Kokuga land, and power.

Toward the end of the Kamikura period, the Houjou family began to occupy a greater and greater percentage of the nation's governor posts. This monopolization of power aroused unrest from other vassals, ultimately leading to the downfall of the Houjou, and indeed, the end of the Kamikura Bakufu.

**In the case of Jito, they would intentionally withhold annual tribute to Kokuga and manor stewards, then as a "solution" agree to pay a fraction of the owed tribute and oversee a section of the land at their expense, thereby acquiring portions of these manors and Kokuga estates and gradually usurping influence from the imperial court and aristocracy. Meanwhile, governors were to able to extend military influence beyond their true means by reappointing Jito and Kokuga to the lowly bureaucratic post of hikan.

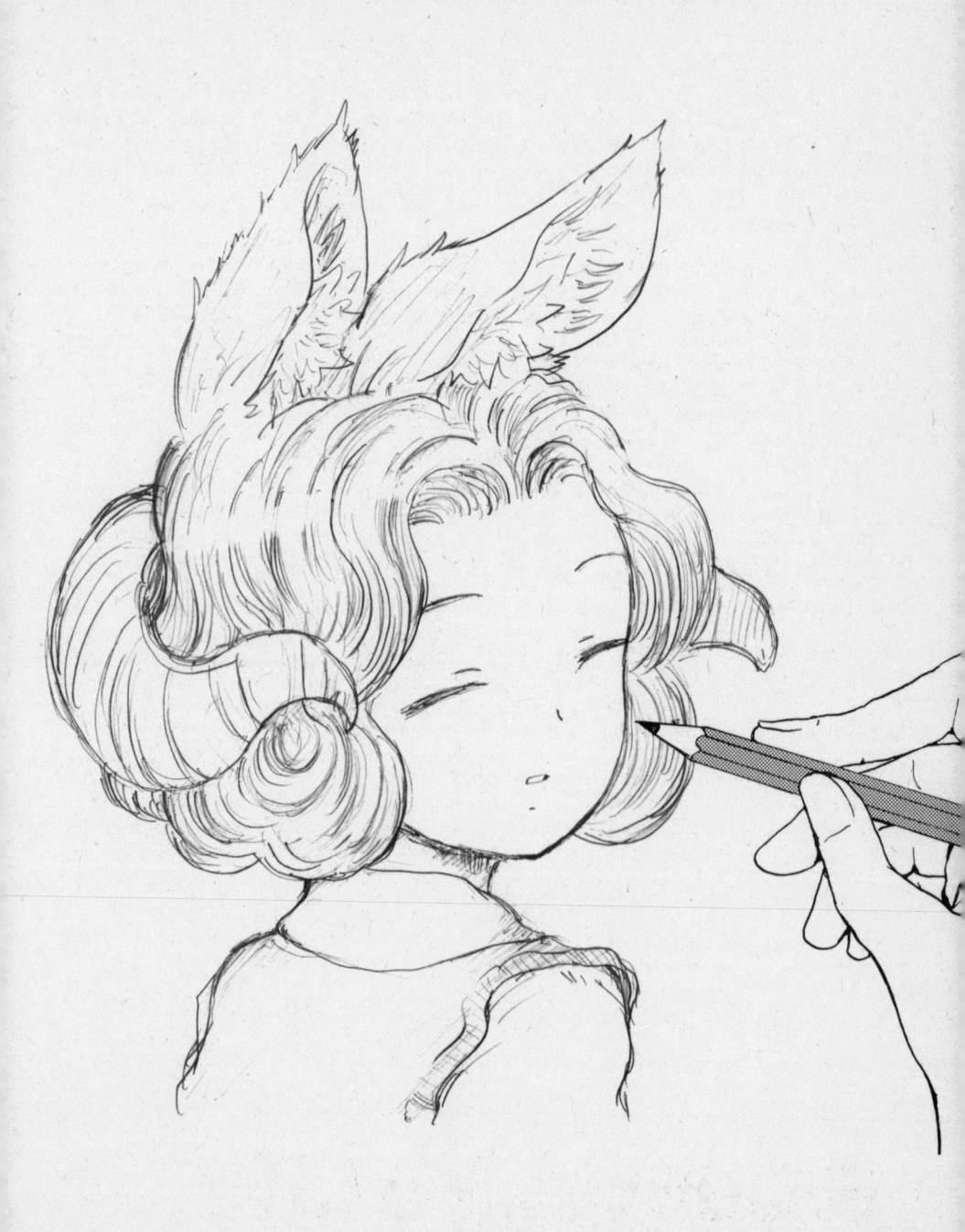

A Centaur's Life

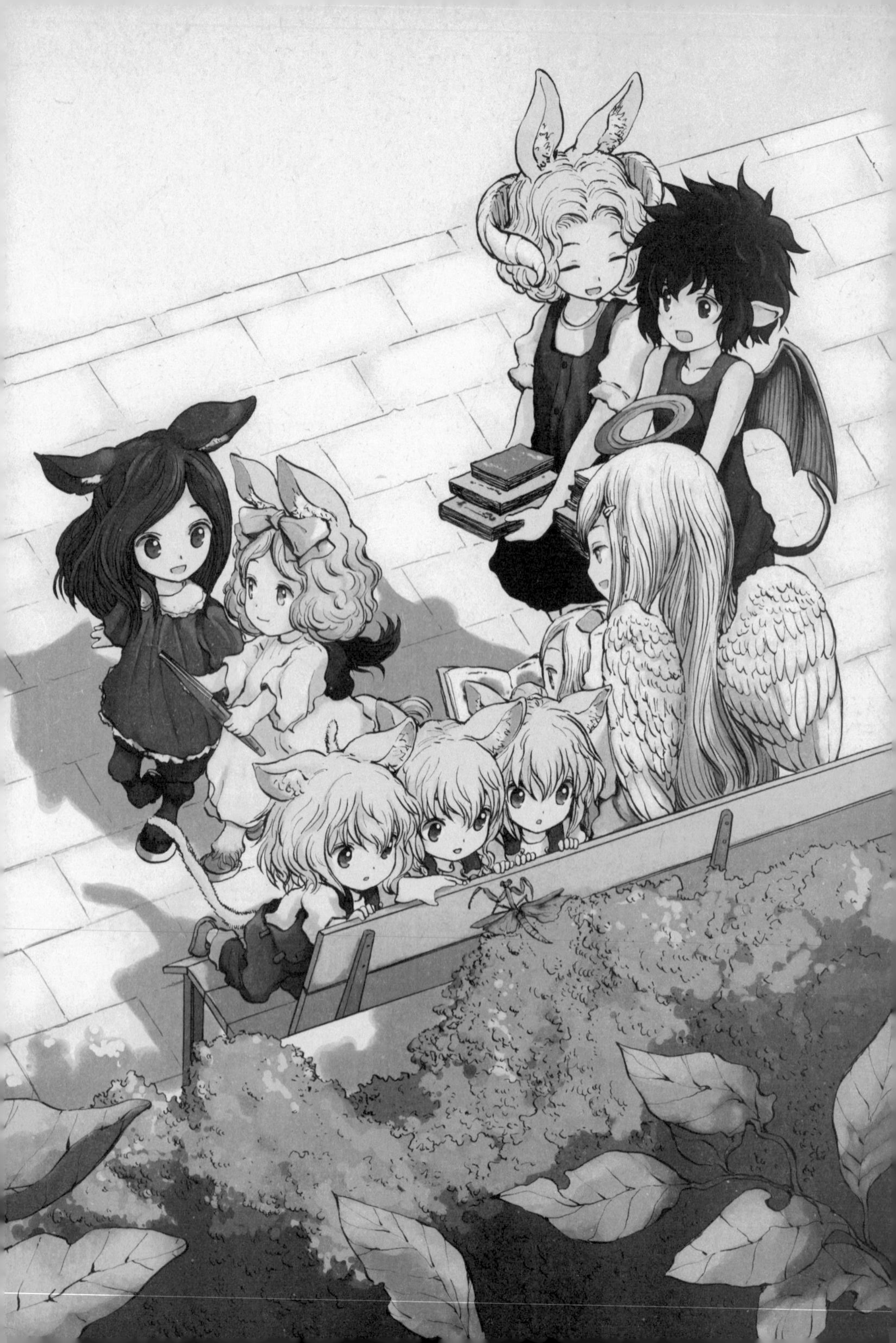

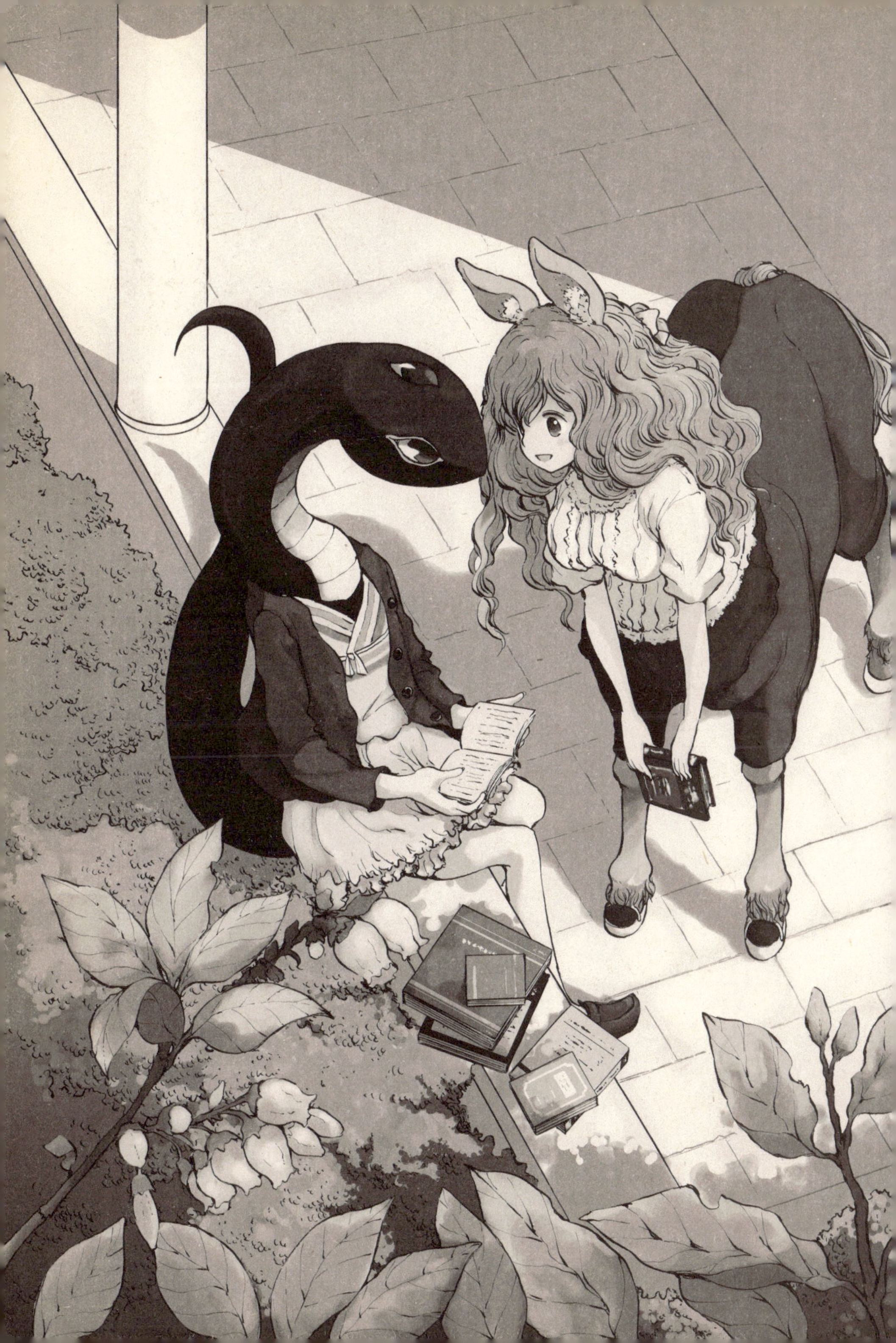

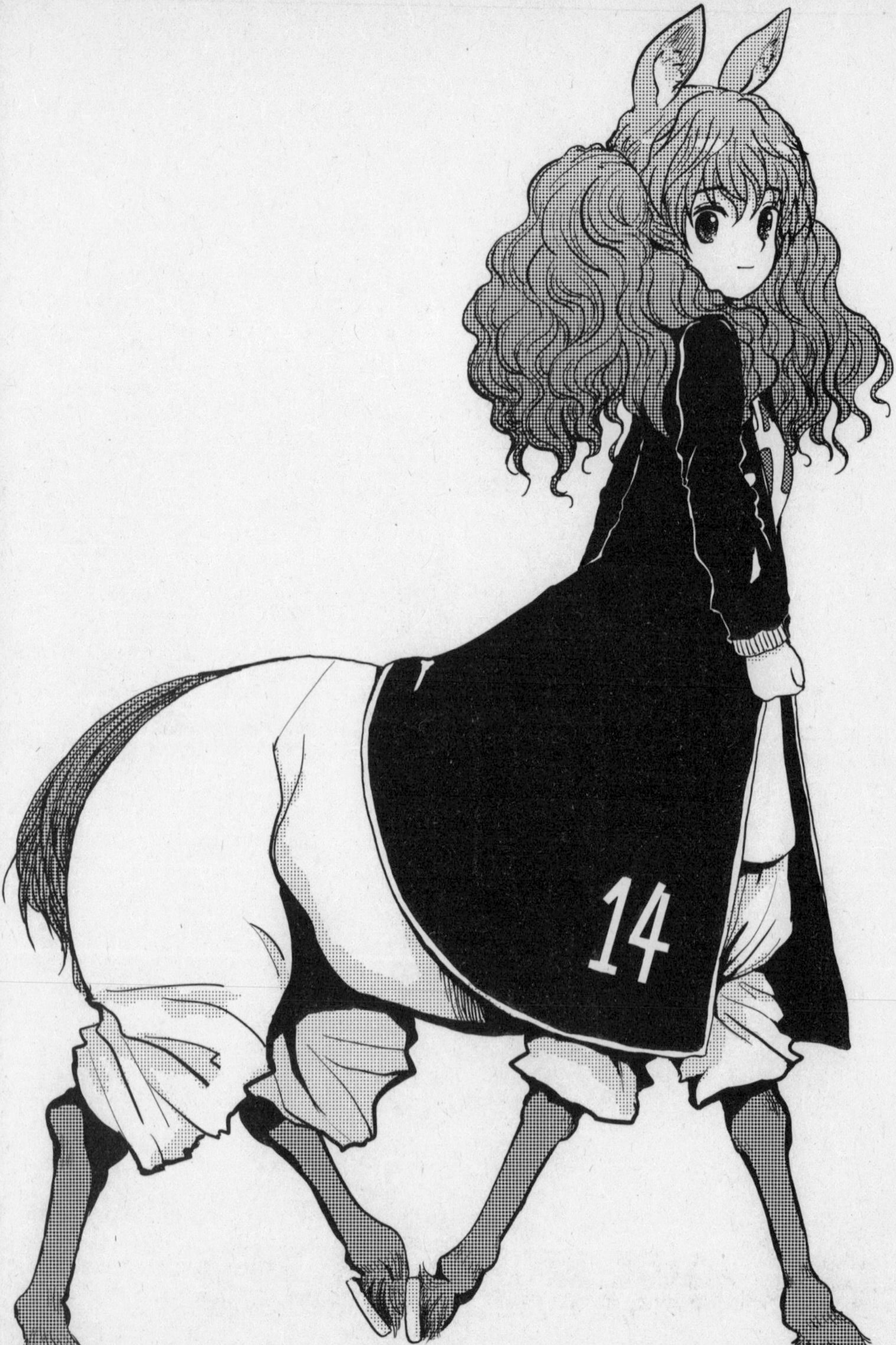
14

A Centaur's Life

Experience all that SEVEN SEAS has to offer!

Visit us Online and follow us on Twitter!
WWW.GOMANGA.COM
WWW.TWITTER.COM/GOMANGA